BP

SU

73

D0864927

LLYFRGELLOEDD BWRDEISTREF SIROL
RHONDDA-CYNON-TAF

DISCARDED
DIFETHWYD

RHONDDA-CYNON-TAFF
COUNTY BOROUGH LIBRARIES

SPECIAL MESSAGE TO READERS

This book is published under the auspices of

THE ULVERSCROFT FOUNDATION

(registered charity No. 264873 UK)

Established in 1972 to provide funds for research, diagnosis and treatment of eye diseases. Examples of contributions made are: —

A Children's Assessment Unit at Moorfield's Hospital, London.

•

Twin operating theatres at the Western Ophthalmic Hospital, London.

•

A Chair of Ophthalmology at the Royal Australian College of Ophthalmologists.

•

The Ulverscroft Children's Eye Unit at the Great Ormond Street Hospital For Sick Children, London.

You can help further the work of the Foundation by making a donation or leaving a legacy. Every contribution, no matter how small, is received with gratitude. Please write for details to:

**THE ULVERSCROFT FOUNDATION,
The Green, Bradgate Road, Anstey,
Leicester LE7 7FU, England.
Telephone: (0116) 236 4325**

**In Australia write to:
THE ULVERSCROFT FOUNDATION,
c/o The Royal Australian and New Zealand
College of Ophthalmologists,
94-98 Chalmers Street, Surry Hills,
N.S.W. 2010, Australia**

AN IMITATION OF LOVE

Catherine Willoughby's brother, Jimmy, has been providing forged documents to help the mysterious 'Captain' assist prisoners escaping from Revolutionary France. When Jimmy is murdered, Catherine and her sister, Alyssa, become wards of Xander Oakley, a dandy whom Catherine despises. Both Catherine and Xander have their secrets, including the love they're beginning to feel for each other. When Catherine runs away, she heads straight into danger. Can Xander save her before it's too late to reveal what's in his heart?

SALLY QUILFORD

◆

AN IMITATION OF LOVE

Complete and Unabridged

LINFORD
Leicester

First published in Great Britain in 2011

First Linford Edition
published 2012

Copyright © 2011 by Sally Quilford
All rights reserved

British Library CIP Data

Quilford, Sally.
    An imitation of love. - -
    (Linford romance library)
    1. Love stories.
    2. Large type books.
    I. Title II. Series
    823.9'2–dc23

    ISBN 978–1–4448–1072–1

Published by
F. A. Thorpe (Publishing)
Anstey, Leicestershire

Set by Words & Graphics Ltd.
Anstey, Leicestershire
Printed and bound in Great Britain by
T. J. International Ltd., Padstow, Cornwall

This book is printed on acid-free paper

1

Catherine Willoughby tiptoed to the window and peered out into the early dawn light. She could see her elder brother, James Willoughby, mounting his horse and, next to him, already seated on a black stallion, the man they called The Captain.

Catherine felt her heart thrill, despite the fact that the Captain's face was covered, and she had no idea what he looked like. Despite the rumours that he was the lowly son of a tradesman, most of the women in England were madly in love with him.

'He is a 'bit of rough', but with a noble heart,' one excited, and very married, female neighbour had whispered to Catherine only recently. 'Imagine what such a man would be like . . . ' Then, suddenly remembering she was talking to a nineteen-year-old unmarried girl, the neighbour had clamped her mouth shut.

Though innocent in many ways, Catherine had not really needed the woman to finish the sentence. She too had her fantasies about the Captain, many of which included him rescuing her from danger, before declaring his undying love with an ardent kiss. She opened the window slightly, hoping to get a better look at him, or to at least hear his voice.

'Did you finish the documents?' she heard the Captain ask in muffled tones. He wore a scarf wrapped around the lower half of his face, and his wide, brimmed hat was tilted forward over his eyes.

'Yes,' answered James, handing over the papers. 'All here. They are perfect. If I may say so myself.'

The Captain perused the documents, and although Catherine could not see it, she felt sure he smiled beneath his mask. 'Good job, old boy. I may be mistaken, but your talent for forgery seems to be growing by the day.'

Momentarily, the Captain glanced up at the house and appeared to see her at her bedroom window. He bowed his head gallantly, then turned his horse and galloped away.

In a few hours, James and the Captain would reach Dover, before sailing across the Channel to save more British prisoners from Napoleon.

Catherine wished them God speed in her heart, and closed the bedroom window. She climbed back into bed and laid her head on the pillow, thinking of the Captain. Even though she realised it was dangerous, she wished he was aware of her part in his mission.

* * *

'Was that one of your sisters at the window?' Alexander Oakley asked James Willoughby as they rode towards Dover.

'Yes — it was Catherine.'

'Really, Jimmy, you should take more care. What if she saw my face?'

'You have nothing to worry about with Cat, Xander. She's on our side. Besides, she's not a blabbermouth. Not like some women. My younger sister, Alyssa, would be a different matter. I've never known anyone say so much about so little.'

'All women love to talk, Jimmy. 'Tis in their nature. If Miss Willoughby found out I was the Captain, she'd break her neck to tell her friends.'

'No, believe me. Cat would not. She has too much at . . . ' James stopped.

'Too much what?'

'Too much common sense. Honestly, had it not been for Cat I know not how I should have survived after the old man died. The estate was almost bankrupt because of his gambling debts. It was Cat who got it back on its feet again. She's far cleverer than I.'

'She's a woman, and I don't trust them. At least, not with a mission as important as ours.'

'I take it you do not discuss our exploits with Mrs Somerson, then.' Mrs

Somerson was a widow recently come to Court, who had set her sights on Xander Oakley the moment her old husband had died.

'I discuss nothing with Phoebe. If I want intelligent conversation, I'll go to the Club, not to a woman.'

'Honestly, Xander, you are the bravest, most noble man I know. But I shall never understand what it is that made you so cynical about women.'

'Years of emptying my pockets and my mind in order to . . . *enjoy* their company.' Xander spurred his horse. 'Come, Jimmy, we are wasting time.'

As he rode on, Xander could not stop thinking about the girl at the window, with her pretty heart-shaped face, intelligent dark eyes, and the glossy chestnut hair that hung loose on her shoulders. Not that he was fooled by the intelligent eyes. No doubt she would soon be regaling her friends with the tale of seeing the Captain. If his previous experience was anything to go by, the story would lose nothing in the telling. The number of women he was supposed to have kissed as he saved them from France had reached double figures — not to mention the few who hinted at him having stolen further pleasures from them.

It was a part of his mission that he hated. It was important to remain anonymous, but it had also led to a mythology about him with which he was not completely comfortable. If he'd kissed and made love to half the women he was supposed to, he would never have time to rescue the prisoners, not to mention how ridiculous an idea it was that, whilst on the run from the French, he'd risk wasting time or shedding his disguise long enough to do either of those things. No; women had stupid notions, and he could not bring himself to believe the young girl at the window was any different.

As soon as he returned from France, he would call on Phoebe Somerson. Her prattling on about love would soon remind him why he remained a bachelor. But for some reason, instead of Phoebe's attractive face, all he could see was a pair of intelligent eyes gazing from a bedroom window.

★ ★ ★

'Cat?' James entered the study, where Catherine sat poring over the accounts. 'Where are the new documents?'

Several weeks had passed since his last trip to France.

'In the safe, dearest. Are you leaving with the Captain again so soon?'

'No. Cat . . . I've not been entirely honest about these latest documents.'

Catherine looked up with questioning eyes. 'What do you mean?'

'Well . . . ' James ran his fingers through his blond hair. 'The truth is, the Captain's exploits aren't nearly enough to keep us fed. He pays well, as you know, but with the French becoming more aware of him, our trips to France are becoming rarer. So . . . well . . . I managed to get the work

7

from someone else. I'm assured it is a noble cause, dearest.'

'Jimmy, no! You promised. You said it would only ever be for the Captain. It is the only reason I agreed.'

'I know, Cat, but . . . well, I'm really strapped. Mr Oakley is holding a steeplechase this weekend, and I need a really good horse if I'm to even have a chance of winning. The prize is one thousand guineas. That would keep us for a long time . . . '

'Oh — Mr Oakley!' Catherine sighed. 'I should have known. Honestly, Jimmy, I can't understand why you'd waste time with that . . . that . . . *dandy!* You know how hurt Papa was when you followed Mr Oakley out of the army, especially as you had worked so hard to move up the ranks. If not for old Mr Oakley's influence at Court, your friend would have been drummed out.'

The story of Oakley's insubordination whilst serving in the army was well known, though the exact details were kept secret — no doubt, Catherine thought, due to his late father's influence. 'I would have hoped that having someone like the Captain as your mentor, you'd start to see what a fool Oakley is. All he cares about is clothes and horses. And women. Though I gather he doesn't much care about the latter, except as just another sport.'

James' eyes widened. 'Cat! I hardly think you should be discussing that. In fact, I cannot begin to think how you know these things. I am afraid I did the wrong thing, involving you in all this.'

'It is a bit late to worry for my mortal soul now, Jimmy,' returned Cat quietly. 'How do you know you can trust these new clients? The Captain has a noble cause, but how do you know these people are not using the documents for more nefarious means?'

'They assure me their cause is impeccable, Cat, but beyond that I did not ask. What we do not know cannot hurt us.'

'Jimmy, dearest, have you ever thought of *not* trying to keep up with

Mr Oakley? He's probably the richest man in England. You — *we* — can't afford his lifestyle. Alyssa should be coming out this year, but you know that is not going to happen now.'

'No, I know, and you missed your coming out completely. I'm sorry, Cat.'

'That's not your fault, darling. Father left us in such a mess.'

'Perhaps if these people offer more work, and pay us for it, you and Alyssa could both come out. You're both extremely pretty girls. You'd be sure to get rich husbands.'

'I've told you before, Jimmy, I have no wish whatsoever to sell myself into a loveless marriage.'

'Nearly all society marriages are loveless, and they manage quite well.'

'Yes, and the husband takes a mistress as soon as possible. Then when the wife has produced an heir and several spares, she takes a discreet lover. That is not what I want. I want . . . '

Catherine realised that Jimmy was so indoctrinated into society, he would never understand. She wished to be loved by someone who never wanted to look at another woman, and to love in return a man who made all other men pale in significance. Failing that, she would rather die an old maid.

'You think I don't understand, but I do,' said Jimmy. 'And believe it or not, Cat, it's what I want too. We are not so different, you and I. But Alyssa is not so choosy. She would quite happily marry the first rich man who paid her any attention.'

'Yes, I know she would. And if that is what she wants, then we will let her make her debut. But not me, Jimmy. I will not parade myself like some prize filly at a racetrack.'

'So you agree to us taking on this new business?'

'Yes, I suppose so. But be careful, Jimmy. Not everyone is as honourable as the Captain.'

★ ★ ★

Several weeks later, standing at James' grave, whilst the rain poured and Alyssa sobbed loudly beside her, Catherine's words came back to haunt her. How could it have happened, when they had been so careful?

She remembered the awful night and the loud knock at the door when the new clients came to collect the documents. Raised voices, James shouting, 'I swear I am alone here! My sisters are staying with relatives.' Then the pistol shot and the sound of horses racing away. She had dashed downstairs to find him lying dead in the hallway, his handsome young face twisted in an agony she could not put from her mind.

Catherine looked across the open grave to where Mr Oakley stood. His face was a bleak mask, and whilst she had no particular regard for him, she could see that her brother's death had hit him hard. *Well, so it should*, she thought bitterly. Had James not been so keen to keep up with Oakley's lifestyle, then none of this would have happened. To die for the Captain's cause would have been one thing. But to die for people who might have more evil intentions was another.

Despite her anger, she had to admit he was a very striking man. She had never actually met him, because he never visited Willoughby Manor, no doubt preferring the more luxurious houses of his richer friends to the ramshackle Elizabethan manor in which the Willoughbys lived. She had imagined him to look soft, plump and pampered, like the Prince of Wales, whom she had once seen from a distance when he visited the North.

The man standing opposite her was tall and lean. His features, far from being conventionally handsome, were rugged, and he had piercing blue eyes under hawk-like brows. He was dressed expensively, and had an expertly tied cravat, but with his broad, powerful shoulders, he was more masculine than she had imagined him to be. There was a rough edge to him that suggested he was not quite the dandy Catherine had believed.

'What will we do?' asked Alyssa, as they walked back to Willoughby Manor. Mr Oakley, and his friend, Mr Andrew Harrington, a good-looking young man of about twenty-four, walked several paces behind them, as if understanding their need for sisterly solitude.

'I won't have my coming out or my pretty dresses now, will I, Cat?'

It was just like Alyssa to worry more about that than whether or not they'd be able to eat for longer than a few weeks before the money ran out. Whoever killed Jimmy had failed to pay him for the forged documents, so they were even worse off than before. Not that Catherine would have wanted to use such money. There was only a little left over from the Captain's fee. Jimmy's funeral had taken much of it.

Catherine had spent the first few hours after Jimmy's death trying to work a way around it. At first she thought she might try and contact the

Captain, to seek his help, but then she had a better idea. After all, the Captain was not a rich man, but Mr Oakley was — and Catherine, in her anger and grief, believed he owed them something for Jimmy's loss.

'I am sure something will turn up, dearest,' said Catherine. 'But if not, you and I can live quite happily as long as we are sensible.'

'I'm tired of being sensible,' said Alyssa, jerking away from her sister. Her beautiful face became petulant. 'I'm seventeen, Cat. I'm supposed to be going to parties and having men fall wildly in love with me. I know you think I am selfish, and not really thinking of Jimmy, and perhaps I am selfish. But I am also thinking of you, Cat. If I married someone very rich then I could take care of you, just as you have always taken care of me and Jimmy.'

'I would never ask you to sacrifice yourself to marriage for me, dearest.'

'But I don't care like you do, Cat. I'm not the falling-in-love type. I want pretty things, and for lots of men to think I'm beautiful.'

What Alyssa said very much echoed what Catherine and James had always known about her. In many ways, Alyssa was probably more realistic than they were about the expectations of women in society. She knew what was expected of her because of her beauty, and was quite happy to use it to her advantage.

'I don't care whether the man I marry loves me or if I love him. So, really, we would not be fooling anyone — and I would finally be able to do my bit for this family. Because I have always hated that you and Jimmy were the clever ones who took care of me.'

'I had no idea you felt that way.'

'No — because you think that I am incapable of thinking of anyone but myself, and I accept that is true most of the time. But whilst I may never love a man, Cat, I do love you — and I loved Jimmy.' Her voice broke a little at the mention of her brother's name. 'That is the only love that matters to me. What our family feel for each other. Even Papa, with all his problems, knew that. He used to say to me, 'However many admirers you get, and you shall have lots with your beautiful face, always remember that your family are the only people who love you for yourself.'

Catherine put her arm around her sister's shoulders and drew her in. 'I am so very proud of you,' she said. 'It will make things much easier.'

'What things?'

'You'll see.' Catherine stole a glance back at Mr Oakley, wondering how much he'd heard of the conversation. What did it matter? If he thought Alyssa was a gold-digger, it would only confirm his views on women. All that mattered was that he would be willing to help them.

An hour later, most of the other guests had gone. Mr Oakley and Mr Harrington remained, talking quietly with the family solicitor, Mr Parry.

'Miss Willoughby, Miss Alyssa,' Mr Parry said eventually. 'I wonder if I might have a word with you in the study? It is about your brother's will.'

'As far as I am aware, Jimmy had nothing to leave,' said Catherine. 'The estate is automatically entailed to our cousin, George.'

'That is what we wish to discuss,' said Mr Oakley. Apart from a few brief words of condolence, it was the most he had said to Catherine all morning.

'What is happening?' asked Alyssa, trembling slightly as Catherine took her hand and led her to the study, where the two men were already waiting.

'I am not sure, dearest,' murmured Catherine. 'But it cannot be anything worse than that which has already happened.'

It was clear who was in charge of proceedings in the study. Mr Parry virtually sank into the background.

'Please take a seat,' Mr Oakley said. Catherine bit back a retort about not needing to be offered a seat in her own house, but remembered that, strictly speaking, it was no longer her home. She seated herself and Alyssa sat next to her, gripping her hand. That Alyssa was overwhelmed by Mr Oakley was unsurprising. Catherine found him frightening, and she was usually the courageous one.

'I am sure,' said Mr Oakley, leaning back on the desk, folding his arms, 'that you have both been very worried for your future. I understand that the estate will now go to a distant cousin who, I gather, is on his way to claim it. Regrettably, not in time to attend Mr Willoughby's funeral.' His tone on the latter statement became brittle.

'That is correct,' replied Catherine. 'And in his letter to me, Cousin George made it clear he has no place for me and Alyssa at Willoughby Manor.' It came as no shock to Catherine that her cousin George had behaved in such a way. There had always been bad feeling in the family, mainly due to the money her father had borrowed, then not repaid. Their cousin, perhaps understandably, felt the Willoughbys had cost him enough, so he was not willing to spend anything further on assisting the two girls.

'I understand that you and Miss Alyssa are virtually penniless.'

'Yes.' Catherine put her chin up; as if by doing so, she might suddenly make herself rich and feel less ashamed than she did at that moment. 'We are not sure what we will do now.'

'You have no need to worry,' answered Mr Oakley. 'Just before he died, it seems your brother had some sort of premonition. I received a letter from him. I would have come to your aid sooner, except I have been away and did not read it until I returned home yesterday. Sadly, it came at the same time as news of his death.' His face became a grim mask once more.

'You said there was a letter?' prompted Catherine when Mr Oakley did not speak for a few moments.

'Yes. Mr Willoughby wrote a letter asking that should anything happen to him, I would become the guardian of you and Miss Alyssa. I am assured by Mr

Parry that the letter is legally binding.'

'But not morally, surely?' queried Catherine. 'What I mean is, surely you are not compelled to follow his wishes.'

Catherine was surprised to hear herself speak, but she wanted to give this man a way out. Then perhaps she would not feel the constriction in her chest which she knew was born of shame.

'On the contrary. For reasons I prefer not to share with you, I consider your brother's request both morally and legally binding. You may both come and live at Oakley Castle, where I have arranged for my Aunt Harriet to come and chaperone you. So, Miss Alyssa,' Oakley bowed in Alyssa's direction, 'you shall have your pretty dresses and make your debut when your proper period of mourning has passed, and I am sure that every man there will fall in love with you.' His tone changed and he became more businesslike. 'Well, we may as well leave here today, before your cousin has a chance to turf you out.' His lips closed into a tight line, suggesting that he did not much approve of Cousin George.

'Oh, this is wonderful!' Alyssa clapped her hands. 'I mean, it is awful about poor Jimmy, but wonderful that he thought of us. Is it not, Catherine?'

'Yes,' agreed Catherine, who was blushing at the realisation that Oakley had heard what Alyssa said on the way back from the churchyard. 'Dearest, why don't you go and pack, and I will discuss the details with Mr Oakley?'

Alyssa did not need telling twice. Catherine could see that her young head was already full of the joys of new dresses, attending balls and having handsome men dance attendance on her.

'Mr Oakley, sir,' she said, when Alyssa had gone, and Mr Parry had also excused himself. 'I hope you will not think ill of my sister. She is very young and, as she believed she might not be able to make her debut, it is something she is very excited about.'

'I believe your sister has a very pragmatic view of life, Miss Willoughby.

She seems to understand exactly how society works.'

'I do not believe that to be true,' said Catherine, hotly. She hated that he might think Alyssa was like some of the mercenary ladies in the Beau Monde, even if Alyssa had done much to give him that impression. 'Alyssa has been shut up at Willoughby Manor for most of her life. She is a complete innocent. She reads about the ladies in society, and believes that she wants to be like them, having no true understanding of the politics of . . . of love.'

Oakley's eyes crinkled with amusement. 'And you, Miss Willoughby, know all about the politics of love?'

'I know that it is not nearly as glamorous as Alyssa believes. That being a wife involves other duties that she probably has not considered.' Catherine blushed again. She had always spoken openly to her brother about anything and everything, and it was only now that she wondered if such a discussion was appropriate with Mr Oakley.

'Yet you are happy for her to make her debut in this society that you seem to despise so much?'

'I want Alyssa to be cared for, and as we are both unable to make our living in this world, then I must concede that finding her a wealthy husband is the only way of ensuring that.'

'And what about you, Miss Willoughby? I shall have to find you a wealthy husband too if I am to do my duty as your guardian.'

'I am not interested in marrying. At least, not in the way Alyssa is content to be married. The reason I wanted to speak to you alone was to assure you that you have no need to introduce me to society at all. I shall be quite content if I can take my books and my easel with me to your home, and then when Alyssa is married, I'm sure she will allow me to live with her, and I shall no longer be a burden to you.'

He bowed his head gallantly. 'I consider you a very charming burden.'

2

Xander had not lied about finding Catherine Willoughby a charming burden. Something about her intrigued him. Most women of her age would be fluttering their eyelashes at him, desperate to become Mrs Oakley. Catherine always met his gaze calmly, and during her first few days at Oakley Castle, he had learned that she was very intelligent.

She was also very stubborn, which was why he was presently searching the grounds for her. He had not seen her for six months, having left his Aunt Harriet to take care of the Misses Willoughbys' needs whilst he dealt with problems in France, where the revolution was causing untold misery.

Despite the length of time that had passed, he was surprised to find that Catherine was still dressed in mourning. He found her sitting under an oak tree, lost in concentration at her easel. Even as he walked towards her, in full view, he was aware, and somewhat intrigued, to realise that she had not even noticed him.

Although everyone agreed that her sister, Miss Alyssa, was the stunningly beautiful sister, Catherine had something else. Something indefinable. To Xander, and many other men, Alyssa was like the sun. Shining and bright, but if one gazed for too long one's eyes began to hurt and the onlooker was forced to look away. Catherine was more like the moonlight, soft and shimmering, and not nearly so painful on the eyes.

'May I see it?' He gestured to the painting. She looked up, startled.

'Mr Oakley!' she exclaimed. 'I did not realise you were there.'

'I gathered that. So, may I see what you have made of my house?'

'No, not yet.' She became a little flustered, quickly covering the canvas with her scarf. He imagined it was because the painting was very bad and she knew it. 'What I mean is, I wish to surprise you with it. You have such a beautiful house. I always thought Willoughby Manor the most wonderful home in Britain, but Oakley Castle is exquisite. So I wanted to paint it, then give the painting to you. A gift, to thank you for all you have done for Alyssa. She cannot wait to make her debut, now she has so many beautiful gowns.'

'It is on that matter that I wished to speak to you.'

'Have we spent too much? I know it seems a lot, and I have urged Alyssa to be more circumspect, but — '

Xander held up his hand. 'That is not important. Miss Alyssa may have as many gowns as she pleases. So may you. This is why I wished to speak to you. I gather from the dressmaker that you have ordered only two black dresses for yourself.'

'I have already told you that I have no wish to be presented to society.'

'But society may come to you.'

She looked up at him, wide-eyed. 'What do you mean?'

'I realise you do not wish to be presented at court, but I intend to invite guests here to stay beforehand, as part of your sister's coming out, so that she has a chance to learn how to behave in society before being thrust into the limelight. Do you think you are doing Miss Alyssa any favours by dressing like a servant?' His eyes took in the cheap black muslin dress Catherine wore. 'Or that any man would be impressed by a woman when her sister's clothes are threadbare?'

He saw her hands go instinctively to a patch on her sleeve.

'I would rather not take too much from you. At least, not for myself,' she answered defensively.

'But you must see how that reflects on Miss Alyssa. And not just on her, but on me, too.'

'On you?' Catherine looked startled.

'I am the legal guardian to you both. What does it say about me, that I keep one sister in style and the other in rags? People might even consider that I favour Miss Alyssa for other reasons.'

He watched her face as his words sank in, just as he intended. In truth he doubted his friends, who knew him well, would think any such thing, but he was determined that Catherine should stop denying herself pretty clothes.

'May I tell the dressmaker to visit you?' he asked.

'Yes. Yes, of course,' replied Catherine, quietly.

'I shall be very angry if I find out that you have ordered anything less than an entire wardrobe.'

'I am not afraid of you, Mr Oakley,' she asserted, her mouth turning up slightly at the corner.

'Well you should be. I'm told I am ferocious.'

To his surprise, she laughed. 'Hardly. You have been so very kind to both of us. Kinder than I ever — '

'Than you ever what?'

'Kinder than I'm sure Jimmy expected.

He probably thought you might just put us in a cottage somewhere and pay the rent.'

'Mr Willoughby knew me better than that.' His voice became grim as he thought of his young friend. If any of them were to die, he expected it to be for the cause. Not knocked down on one's own doorstep by a group of murderous vagabonds. 'I wish to talk to you about Jimmy. I have not wanted to say anything sooner, because I know his loss affected you deeply. As it did me. But we must find out who murdered him. I know the local authorities have put it down to vagabonds in the area, but I am not convinced. Do you know anything about the men who came to the house that night?'

Catherine shook her head. 'No, I am afraid not. It was all so quick.'

He seated himself on a tree stump beside her easel. 'Do you know of any reason why they might have been there? Perhaps Jimmy had debts.'

'He did have debts; those Papa left us

with, but most of them had been paid off. The people we owed money to were tradesmen. Not the type to send men around.'

Xander knew that to be true. He had always paid Jimmy over the odds for the forged documents, determined to do something to help his proud friend.

'Did he ever discuss anyone else with whom he might be involved? I've heard, though it may just be a rumour, that Jimmy knew the Captain.'

'Oh, but the Captain did not do this! He and Jimmy were true friends. He would never harm him, I know it.'

'No, I am not suggesting he did,' said Xander, feeling unaccountably jealous about Catherine's passionate defence of his alter-ego. 'But it may have some bearing. Do you know what Jimmy did for the Captain?'

Catherine appeared to hesitate. 'I am afraid to tell you, in case it makes you think less of Jimmy.'

'Believe me when I tell you that I hold, and will continue to hold, your brother in the highest esteem. I know how much he cherished you and Miss Alyssa, and how he desired to release you all from the penury you suffered after your father left you all penniless. Believe it or not, I have offered to help in the past, but Jimmy was too proud to take it.'

'Did you? I knew he was proud. I did not know you had offered.'

'I imagine Jimmy was also too proud to admit it. But we are getting off the subject. You must tell me everything you know. Do you know who the Captain is?' He regarded her face intently.

Catherine shook her head. 'No. I have only seen him from a distance and then his face was covered.'

'Jimmy never hinted at who he might be?'

'Never. I suppose I should tell you the truth. It matters little now Jimmy is dead. The Captain relied on Jimmy because of his talent for forgery.'

'Forgery?'

'Oh, now you are going to . . . '

Xander held up his hand. 'No, I am not shocked. Only surprised that you should know about it. Jimmy once told me about how he forged notes from your father to get out of lessons at school.'

Catherine laughed a little. 'Yes, he did. Then he put it to less selfish uses. Whenever the Captain needed forged documents to get into France, Jimmy provided them for him. Then . . . '

'What?' He leaned forward.

'Someone else found out about Jimmy's talent, and they offered him a lot of money. I was not happy, but Jimmy said it would help Alyssa to have her season in London. I should never have agreed . . . '

'You think the men who killed him were something to do with that?'

Catherine nodded. 'Yes. I think that, for whatever reason, they silenced him. They might have hurt me and Alyssa, too, but I heard Jimmy tell them we were away visiting relatives. Then they . . . ' She put her hands to her face. 'It is all my fault. I should never have . . . '

'Miss Willoughby, listen to me.' Xander gently removed her hands from her stricken face and held them in his. 'It is not your fault. It was foolish of Jimmy to get involved with other . . . clients beside the Captain. Do you know anything about them? Even the names on the forged documents might help. I don't suppose Jimmy shared that with you.'

'No,' she said brokenly. 'No, he did not. I think Alyssa wants me.'

Abruptly Catherine got up from her chair and rushed off towards the house. He expected to see Alyssa on the terrace, but no one was there.

She was hiding something, Xander was sure of it. But what?

He was about to follow her, when he bumped into the easel, knocking it to the ground. The scarf fell away, revealing her painting of Oakley Castle.

'Good Lord,' exclaimed Xander, hardly able to believe his eyes. It was not a poor painting at all. He would go so far as to say it was excellent. Admittedly it owed a lot to Gainsborough. All that was missing was a gentleman and his lady in the foreground. In fact, had Miss Willoughby been a less honourable young lady, she might even have passed it off as a Gainsborough original.

*   *   *

Catherine barely noticed what gowns she picked as the dressmaker bustled around her, obviously delighted to have the extra business. She was too busy thinking about Jimmy and whether she could really trust Mr Oakley. Even in the short time she had spent in his company, she had begun to wonder if she had been wrong about him. He had been more generous than he ever needed to be, both to herself and to Alyssa. What was more, she had enjoyed talking to him at dinner, finding him very knowledgeable once he conquered his initial reservations about discussing politics and philosophy with a mere woman.

Even if she told Oakley the names on the forged documents, what could he do about it? They might have been used by now, assuming Jimmy's killers had achieved their aim. But why would they need to kill Jimmy first? If all they planned to do was leave the country and take on new identities, then there would be no reason to silence him.

Unless what they planned was something different. Something they feared might come to light before they achieved it. And if that were the case, did she not have a duty to let Mr Oakley know so that he could inform the proper authorities? Added to which, she did want Jimmy's killers brought to justice — and it might be the only way to do it.

On the other hand, if she told him what she knew, it might lead to other questions, such as how she came to know so much. It could lead to her and

Alyssa being thrown out onto the streets. She had a feeling that Mr Oakley was not a man who would take kindly to being deceived.

It was strange how he had appeared at her side whilst she was painting. Engrossed in her work, she had been unaware of him walking towards her, yet the moment she knew he was there, she became acutely aware of him, to the point that her heart beat faster and she lost her normal cool reserve. In his company, she felt as dizzy as Alyssa. She only hoped he had not noticed it. She would hate for him to think of her as a simpering young female. Though she doubted he thought much of her at all.

'I will leave you these gowns, Miss Willoughby,' the middle-aged dress-maker was saying, 'and bring you more tomorrow.'

'Thank you,' murmured Catherine absently, barely looking at the gowns the dressmaker had laid carefully on the bed.

'And, may I say, it has been a pleasure dressing you. Your sister is beautiful, but you have something else about you. To see my clothes on you is like . . . Oh, I cannot explain. Like seeing a portrait in its proper frame.'

Catherine was surprised. 'That is a very kind thing to say. Thank you.'

'I must admit I hated to see you dressed in mourning, especially when there is no need any more. It is such a waste of a beautiful young lady.'

'Stop!' said Catherine, holding up her hand and laughing. 'You will make me very conceited.'

'I do not think there is much chance of that, Miss Willoughby.'

'Do you make Mr Oakley's clothes too?'

'Lors, no. He has a tailor in London for that. But I have sometimes . . . ' The dressmaker clamped her lips shut as if she'd said too much.

'Yes?' Catherine raised her eyebrows inquiringly.

'It's nothing I should discuss with a

nice young lady like yourself . . . ' Then, as if she couldn't help herself, 'But sometimes Mr Oakley might buy a dress for a lady friend. Like Mrs Somerson. Though she turned her nose up at my dresses.' The dressmaker sniffed. 'Only Paris fashions are good enough for her. Not that she will get many of them, with things the way they are.'

'Mrs Somerson is coming this weekend, I believe.' Catherine felt her heart sink. She had heard from Aunt Harriet that Mr Oakley was besotted with the beautiful young widow.

'So I hear,' the woman agreed.

'In that case, Miss Alyssa and I will wear your beautiful clothes with pride,' said Catherine, smiling, 'and show her what she is missing.'

At that the dressmaker's eyes filled with tears of gratitude. 'What a lovely young lady you are. 'Tis a pity that Mr Oakley . . . ' Again she stopped and despite Catherine's entreaties, refused to be drawn into further discussion.

When Catherine entered the dining room later that evening, dressed in a gown of pale blue silk, Alyssa ran towards her, delighted. 'Oh, darling, you look so pretty! Does she not, Mr Oakley? Mr Harrington?'

Mr Oakley stood up and bowed. 'I fear that with the two Miss Willoughbys and Aunt Harriet,' he bowed to his aunt, already seated on account of her age, 'we are surrounded by far too much beauty for mere mortals, Andrew,' he said.

Aunt Harriet twittered slightly. It had occurred to Catherine some months before that in bringing his aunt to Oakley Castle, Mr Oakley had not only done Catherine and Alyssa a good turn, he had also helped his aunt. She had been widowed at around the same time Jimmy died, and was left with very little income. It was also noticeable how everyone called her Aunt Harriet, even Catherine, Alyssa and Mr Harrington.

The lady seemed to enjoy the title, perhaps because she had very few relatives apart from Mr Oakley, and she liked to think of herself as being part of a family.

'You are hardly a mere mortal, Mr Oakley,' observed Catherine, as he held out her chair for her. She felt sure he was only teasing her about being beautiful, when Alyssa, dressed all in white; was a vision of sheer loveliness.

Mr Harrington helped Alyssa into her chair. He was clearly already besotted with her. But Catherine had been told that his family was almost as impoverished as the Willoughbys. If Alyssa was to be cared for, then she needed a much richer beau. Catherine felt a little ashamed about being so mercenary, then reminded herself that Alyssa also understood that and was quite content with it.

'I have heard it said you can walk on water,' she said to Mr Oakley.

'Now you are teasing me, Miss Willoughby.'

'No, I have never seen him walk on water. Seen him fall into the Channel a few times,' joked Mr Harrington as he took his own seat.

'I do not need to come to my own home to be insulted,' returned Mr Oakley. 'I have many more places I can visit for that.'

Despite his jocular tone, Catherine sensed an undercurrent, as if he were warning Mr Harrington about something.

'I cannot imagine you have many chances to fall into the Channel nowadays,' said Catherine. 'Is it even safe to cross it?'

'I know I should be terrified,' said Alyssa. 'I am sure the French must be waiting to attack any English boat.'

'I assure you we are ready to fight back, Miss Alyssa,' said Mr Oakley.

'I am told that you both served in the army with dear Jimmy,' said Alyssa. 'You must tell us all about the battles in which you took part.' She was looking at Mr Harrington as she spoke, her eyes full of admiration.

'I am sure you would soon be bored,' said Mr Oakley, with a somewhat cynical tone to his voice. 'And I am sure that young ladies such as yourselves should not be discussing such things.'

'Not at all,' rejoined Catherine. 'Women can be just as interested in great battles as men.' Although, given that Oakley had been forced to resign his commission, she doubted he would have much of a story to tell.

'Is it really true that you were accused of insubordination, Mr Oakley?' asked Alyssa artlessly.

Only Alyssa could get away with asking such a direct question, but even so it took everyone by surprise. Catherine was grateful to her, however, as she was most interested to know the facts of what had happened.

'It is not something of which we speak,' said Aunt Harriet, primly. 'Alexander's father was most annoyed.' Then as if remembering who was feeding her and keeping a roof over her head, she added, 'Though I am sure that Alexander had his reasons.'

'Is it true, Mr Oakley?' asked Catherine.

'It is true,' he said. 'And if I had my time again I'd do exactly the same.'

'What happened?'

'Our Commanding Officer got very drunk one night and decided that a nearby village was harbouring insurgents, despite the fact that we had had no intelligence of the sort. He ordered us to go and 'wake up the natives'. What he intended was a cold-blooded massacre; had we gone, we would have been guilty of an atrocity beyond measure, and for no military benefit. So I ignored the order, hoping that he would forget it once he had sobered up in the morning. Unfortunately he did not.'

Catherine could see the haunted look in his face, as if he was thinking of what might have happened to the innocent villagers. She shivered slightly.

'So Oakley, who had quickly worked

his way up the ranks, was just as quickly busted down to Captain and politely asked to resign his commission,' finished Mr Harrington. 'Several of us, myself and Jimmy included, followed him as a measure of our support.'

'What happened to the Commanding Officer?' asked Catherine. She wondered why Jimmy had never told her the story, instead letting her and their father continue to believe that Mr Oakley had behaved badly, when in fact he had behaved with great courage and nobility. 'Surely he wasn't allowed to continue in his command?'

'He is dead,' said Mr Oakley. Now there was a definite warning note in his voice as he looked at Andrew Harrington. 'But this is not a discussion to be having with two young ladies. I suggest we move on to more cheerful topics. Andrew, I am sure you have some gossip from the Court with which to delight and enthrall our young guests.'

As Mr Harrington kept Alyssa

amused with talk of The Prince of Wales and the court, Catherine kept going back over their earlier conversation, feeling there was something she had missed that might be important.

'Please,' she heard Mr Oakley address her quietly in his warm, deep tones. 'Put it out of your mind. I should never have told you. It is not a proper discussion to be having with two young ladies.'

'I am glad you did,' she replied. 'I must admit that in the past I have held an opinion of you that I now know to be undeserved. I thought you cared for nothing but clothes and . . . ' she was going to say 'women', but hastily substituted, ' . . . horses.'

'Horses?' His raised eyebrow suggested that he knew exactly what she had intended to say.

'Yes. But the kindness you have shown me and my sister, and your courage in defying your Commanding Officer, tells me that you are a very different man. So I owe you an apology.'

'You owe me nothing of the sort.

Sometimes the image we put out to the world is the one we wish for it to see.'

She wondered what exactly he meant by that. As she looked across the table at him, Catherine began to wonder whether, perhaps, she could trust this man after all.

As Mr Harrington amused Alyssa with yet another piece of Court gossip, Mr Oakley leaned across to her and murmured in a low voice, 'If you are wondering whether or not you can trust me, then the answer is yes. We shall talk further tomorrow.'

She glanced down at her meal, feeling unnerved. How could he know her every thought and every feeling?

3

In the event Catherine did not get a chance to talk to Mr Oakley the next day. His guests from London arrived in a convoy of magnificent carriages, and Oakley Castle was a bustle of activity as they were presented and then shown to their rooms.

'Miss Willoughby, Miss Alyssa, I would like you to meet Mrs Somerson,' announced Mr Oakley, as a red-haired beauty climbed the steps to the spot where Catherine and Alyssa waited.

Phoebe Somerson made a beeline for Alyssa. 'Oh, Xander, you were right about her. She is such a doll. I will make you my pet when we go to Court, dear, and ensure only the very best-looking and richest young men talk to you.' She took Alyssa by the arm, and walked into the house with her, virtually ignoring Catherine. Alyssa glanced back, alarmed, clearly not liking the idea of being Phoebe Somerson's pet very much at all.

'My sister, Miss Catherine Willoughby, is also pleased to meet you,' Alyssa said pointedly.

'Oh yes, Miss Willoughby,' said Phoebe, remembering her manners. She held out her hand, which was cold to the touch. 'I think Xander may have mentioned you.'

Rather than being offended, Catherine was amused. She gave a small curtsey. 'Mrs Somerson. I think Mr Oakley may have mentioned you, too,' she answered mischievously.

She noticed Mr Oakley's lips twitch slightly and wondered if he was about to remonstrate with her. Instead, he gestured for Catherine to go into the house with Phoebe and Alyssa, and he followed them.

There was no doubt that Phoebe Somerson already considered Oakley Castle to be hers, and that she was the hostess for the weekend. She had no compunction about standing at Mr Oakley's side as he talked to his guests, taking the honour they showed him as her due. She was charming to everyone, and everyone was charmed by her. Except Catherine, to whom she seemed rather brittle.

Catherine was wise enough to admit to herself that seeing Phoebe Somerson at Oakley's side irked her a little. In a short time she had come to admire him greatly and to understand why Jimmy had done the same. She could not understand why a man of his intelligence and courage would want a woman who seemed to have very little of any importance to say. But, she supposed, he had other reasons for admiring Mrs Somerson. That she was beautiful was without doubt. She would make a fine Mrs Oakley.

In Phoebe Somerson, Catherine also saw what Alyssa might become. Could she bear to see her sister turn into such a mercenary? For the first time she began to wonder whether she had done the right thing in bringing Alyssa to Oakley Castle.

It was too late now. The die was cast. But she hoped that Alyssa might retain some of the genuine humanity that Catherine knew was hidden amongst the love of fine clothes and flattering words from men.

If only Alyssa could marry someone like Mr Oakley! He might inspire her to be a better person. At that thought, Catherine wondered why she had not considered it before. Apart from the fact that Mr Oakley was twelve years older than Alyssa, he would be the perfect choice. So why, when she thought of him with her sister, did Catherine feel even more irritation than she did seeing him with Phoebe Somerson?

The answer came to her in an instant. He had no intentions of ever marrying Phoebe Somerson. She might make a fine Mrs Oakley in regards to her looks, but there was something rather cheap about her manner.

Alyssa, on the other hand, was well brought up and, though young, behaved in the way a noble lady should. Mr

Oakley would never marry Phoebe Somerson — but he might marry someone like Alyssa.

'Are you well, Miss Willoughby?'

She jumped when she realised that, once more, he had crept up on her, but that again she became acutely aware of his presence as soon as he did make it known. 'Oh! I am very well, thank you, Mr Oakley.'

'You looked a little upset. Has anything happened to disturb you?'

'No, not at all. It has been a long day and I am a little tired. We have lived rather a quiet life at Willoughby Manor. I have never been in the presence of so many people before. I feel as if . . . '

'As if what, Catherine?' The tender use of her first name surprised her so much, she had no chance to question whether it was proper. All she knew was that she liked the way he said it in his deep tones.

'I'm being silly. And ungrateful. I'm sorry.'

'You feel as if you would like to

simply run away from them all, and go somewhere quiet by yourself.'

'Yes. How did you know?'

'It is how I sometimes feel. Seeing the same people time after time. Hearing the same gossip. It all gets rather boring. But you are far too new to this to be tired of it yet. You are young and beautiful, and should be surrounded by eager admirers. In fact, I intend to take my friends to task about their lack of manners. I fully expected to be having to warn them all to stop crowding you.'

'I think Alyssa outshines every other woman in the room far too much for that.' She looked across to her sister, who was indeed surrounded by several handsome young men.

'And yet you don't seem to mind? Most women would be vying for attention. Like Mrs Somerson.'

As he said the words, Phoebe Somerson laughed loudly, but without any real humour, drawing all eyes away from Alyssa and to herself.

'I have already intimated to you, I have no wish to enter the marriage market. I just want Alyssa to be happy.'

'And I have told you that you are far too young and beautiful to make that decision. Unless, like many women in this room, you are waiting for the Captain to jump through your window and propose.'

'Now you are mocking me. Besides, from what I hear, the Captain has more than enough admirers.'

'True. It is a wonder he gets anything done.'

Catherine laughed. 'I have often thought the same. And if he kisses every woman he saves, he is clearly not very discerning. But he is very brave and noble, and his cause is a good one.'

'You should beware of fairy stories, Miss Willoughby. Sometimes people are not what the legends say they are.'

'You sound as if you know him.' The thought had not occurred to Catherine before, but she supposed that if Jimmy had known the Captain, then Mr

Oakley might have, too. In fact, he could be in the room now! She scoured the faces of all the men, wondering, before her eyes naturally fell once more upon the gentleman before her.

'I've never met the man,' said Mr Oakley, firmly. 'And I doubt very much whether he is here. He is, by all accounts, the son of a tradesman.'

'Now I am disappointed in you,' retorted Catherine.

'And why should you be?'

'I did not consider you a snob.'

'I am not, but many of the people here are. And whilst they may cheer on the Captain's adventures, I can assure you, he would not be allowed to set foot in their drawing rooms.' There was something harsh about the way he spoke, as if such snobbery mattered to him personally. 'Which reminds me. You and I need to — '

'Xander!' Phoebe Somerson stepped forward and put her hand on Oakley's arm, her pretty lips set in a pout. 'You are neglecting me after I have come all this way. What are you and young Miss Willoughby talking about? Were you teaching her some new nursery rhymes?'

'Actually,' replied Mr Oakley, smiling, 'we were discussing fairy stories.'

Mrs Somerson laughed, obviously relieved. 'Well, I refuse to let you tuck her in. Leave that to the servants. Come, I wish to play your wonderful piano, and you must turn the pages.'

Catherine felt as though she had been slapped. Whilst she did not care what Mrs Somerson thought of her, Mr Oakley's words put her very much in her place. To him she was nothing more than a child. If only he knew the truth! She bit her lip to stop the tears that threatened to fall, wondering why it mattered so much to her. A few weeks ago she had not even liked him.

She glanced up to find him looking down at her, with a quizzical look in his eyes. Phoebe was already on her way to the piano, which stood in the salon adjoining the drawing room.

'Now you are upset,' observed Mr

Oakley softly. 'Why?'

'Xander? You promised to turn the pages,' Mrs Somerson called from the adjoining room.

'I think Mrs Somerson wants you,' was all that Catherine would say.

Xander had trouble concentrating on turning the pages, wondering what on earth had got into Catherine. Everything had been fine until Phoebe had come along. Then it began to dawn on him.

But it couldn't be true — and if it was, he would have to nip it in the bud. He was nearly thirty years old; Catherine only nineteen. What's more, he was her legal guardian and responsible for her welfare. But he would have been a fool if he had failed to notice how her initial coolness with him had turned to admiration. Clearly she was building him up in her mind as some sort of hero because he had helped her and Alyssa, and because of the story he had told the night before. He had not considered how impressionable young

57

girls could be, having spent his time in the company of men or older women.

No, he would have to find a way to descend from the pedestal on which Catherine had clearly placed him. Her admiration was a complication he could not afford, especially if he was to encourage her to marry.

At that thought, he felt himself getting angry. What if he chose the wrong man for her? What if she ended up living a miserable life with a husband who treated her badly? Or with a man who did not understand that, rare amongst women, she liked to discuss topics other than her pretty new bonnet? His duty would only last until the day she married, yet part of him felt that it went beyond that.

It then struck him, like a flash of lightning, that the idea of her being married to anyone else but him was anathema to him.

But he was acutely aware that she was very young, and if he approached her in a romantic way, she might even see it as a betrayal of the trust she had put in him. He would be guilty of taking advantage of a vulnerable young woman who in the course of two short years had lost both her father and her brother, leaving her without a stabilising male influence in her life.

No matter how much she might think she admired him, it could only be puppy love. He had to be the sensible one — though he had to admit that he did not feel very sensible at that moment. It took every ounce of his self-control not to go and find her and tell her how he felt.

The age difference and her vulnerability were not the only reasons. The life he lived, as the Captain, was a dangerous one. It also meant a lot of time travelling that, as a single man, he might be able to explain away to outsiders, but would find far harder to explain to a wife waiting at home. It might also put her in peril if anyone ever found out the truth about him. The thought of her being used to get at him was horrifying.

The more he thought about it, the more insurmountable the problem of Catherine and his feelings for her seemed. There were too many reasons not to tell her he loved her, fighting against his heart which told him that reasons did not matter as long as she married no one else.

'Xander!' chided Phoebe. 'You really are absent-minded tonight.'

'I'm sorry,' he said, turning the page, and realising that everyone had been waiting for him. 'I've rather a lot on my mind.'

'Fairy stories, I suppose,' Phoebe hissed as she played. She smiled at the assembled guests before muttering under her breath. 'The sooner you get these little girls off your hands, the better. Fatherhood doesn't suit you.'

At that harsh reminder of the age difference that had been worrying him, Xander flicked the page over, knowing full well that Phoebe had not yet reached that point in the music, and was not talented enough to remember what the rest of the line should be.

★　★　★

Later that night, Catherine sought the solace of her own bedroom, having claimed a headache, glad to be away from the party downstairs. She had been lying in bed for about half an hour when Alyssa came into the room, dressed in her nightgown, and climbed in beside her. It was something she often did last thing at night, so they could chat about the day.

'Wasn't it a wonderful party, Cat?' Alyssa snuggled down next to her.

'Yes, it was, darling. You had lots of admirers.'

'Mrs Somerson didn't like that one bit. I think she and Mr Oakley have had a row. He barely talked to her after you left, and then he and Mr Harrington went off somewhere on their horses.'

'Really? I wonder why, when he has guests in the house.'

'I don't know. He received a note or something. But Mrs Somerson is not happy about it. Have you seen her maid?'

'No, dearest, I have not.'

'Our maid Jenny says Mrs Somerson's maid is half-French, her name is Celine, and that she's stuck up and always listening at doors.'

'Darling, you know you really shouldn't listen to the servants' gossip.'

'Why not? It's the best sort there is! But what if Mrs Somerson's maid is actually a *spy*?'

'I hardly think so. What would she learn here? There are no battles being planned in this house.'

'Well, no, but what about around the king and The Prince of Wales?'

'I gather from what I hear that he does not much bother himself with the war. He only cares about his parties and lady friends.'

'Mr Harrington said that it is not quite true; the Prince of Wales is far more intelligent than people give him credit for, but that his Majesty does not trust the prince enough to share affairs of state with him. Mr Harrington said . . . ' Alyssa continued in that vein for quite some time, and Catherine couldn't fail to notice quite how much Mr Harrington had said.

'You like him, do you not?' she asked eventually, when Alyssa had stopped to draw breath. 'Mr Harrington, I mean.'

'He has been very kind to me, and helped me to learn how I should behave in society. And it does not hurt to have one handsome man admiring me, does it? It will give all the others something to think about.' Alyssa was silent for a while. 'It's not as if I am falling in love with him, Cat. I know what I have to do to help the family.'

'Oh, darling . . . ' Catherine felt the tears she had been fighting back all day start to fall. Despite Alyssa's protestations, it was clear that she was falling very much in love with Mr Harrington. It was as she had feared. Alyssa was so young and impressionable, and had been shut away with her dreams at Willoughby Manor for so long, it was obvious that the first handsome man who told her she was beautiful would become her first great love.

'And poor people are not happy. Mr Harrington told me that. He said there is a great deal of poverty in London and that he and Mr Oakley help as best they can, but he says it is a bottomless pit. No matter how much money Mr Oakley gives, it is never enough. So when I marry a rich man and become a great lady, I shall be able to help people. It will make me feel better about having things, and not so bad about not being with someone I love.' Alyssa's voice trembled a little. 'See, I am not such a selfish person, am I?'

'No, indeed you are not. You are an angel. I think perhaps I have been mistaken in bringing us here.'

'You? How can you say that, Catherine? If not for you, we would have starved. If you had not . . . '

Catherine put her hand out and

gently covered Alyssa's mouth. 'Careful, dearest, there may be a French maid listening.'

Although Catherine said it as a joke, she was sure she heard someone moving outside the bedroom door. Telling herself she was only imagining things, she nevertheless started to talk in a deliberately louder voice about the party and the clothes everyone had been wearing.

4

Catherine must have dozed, because the next thing she knew, she was awoken by the sound of whispering outside her open window. Her bedroom was at the back of the house, above the kitchens. She crept out of bed carefully, so as not to wake Alyssa, who had decided not to go back to her own room because she had wanted to talk a little more. She looked out to see two men, one of whom seemed to be supporting the other.

'Wait, Xander, while I open the door,' she heard Mr Harrington's voice say. It was then she realised that the stricken man was Mr Oakley.

Gasping in horror, and without thinking what she was doing, Catherine flung on her dressing gown and almost flew down the back staircase, reaching the back door just as Mr Harrington helped Mr Oakley through it.

'Miss Willoughby,' gasped Mr Oakley. 'Go back to bed this instant.' His face was pale, and she saw a patch of blood spreading over his white shirt.

She ignored him and went to his other side to help Mr Harrington, who led them to a small room in which was a single bed, and what appeared to be a medicine chest. Almost as if it was ready for this very purpose.

'What happened?' she asked. 'Who has hurt you?'

'A duel,' answered Mr Oakley, as they helped him onto the bed. His breathing was labored. 'Now go back to bed.'

Mr Harrington lit a candle, casting more light into the room.

'No, I want to help. I sometimes helped Jimmy when . . . ' She paused.

'You can speak in front of Andrew. He knows about Jimmy's association with the Captain.'

'Yes, when he helped the Captain. A few times he came back injured and I nursed him. Why were you fighting a duel?'

'Some young fool made an offensive

comment about Mrs Somerson,' said Mr Oakley, appearing to choose his words carefully. 'So, of course I was obliged to defend her honour.'

'Of course,' murmured Catherine, her heart dropping. 'Who was it? All the young men here tonight seemed very polite.'

'Any one of them can turn when he's had too much wine,' said Mr Harrington darkly. Catherine noticed that neither of them answered her question. She opened the medicine chest and took out some bandages and a bottle of medicinal alcohol.

'Let me see,' she said. Forgetting for a moment with whom she was dealing, she pulled up Mr Oakley's shirt, to see that he had a deep cut in his side. Mr Harrington then helped her remove the shirt completely, so that it did not impede her ministrations. 'You were sword fencing?'

In spite of his pain, he looked surprised. 'Yes. I am most impressed that you can tell a sword wound when you see one.'

'I told you, I helped Jimmy on a number of occasions. I thought the usual way to duel was with pistols.'

'It's up to the duellists which weapons they use. Ouch.' Oakley winced as Catherine cleaned the wound with the alcohol.

'Don't be such a baby,' she admonished. 'If you cannot stand pain, you should not be fighting duels.' She concentrated on making sure there was no dirt in the wound. 'I think I may have to put some sutures in this.'

'You can do that?'

'Jimmy taught me how.'

'He obviously relied on you a lot.'

'Yes, he did.' Catherine's voice wavered.

'Most women would be fainting about this point in proceedings,' said Mr Harrington with a note of admiration in his voice.

'I'm not the swooning kind,' returned Catherine, smiling.

'That much is certain,' groaned Mr Oakley. 'Dear Lord, woman, do you have to be so brutal?' Catherine had started putting the first suture in without warning him.

'I always found it best not to warn Jimmy when I was about to start. He'd make such a fuss otherwise,' she explained. She did wonder if she had been a touch too rough with Mr Oakley. She could not banish the thought that he could have died, defending Phoebe Somerson's honour. He was not an old man, but he was definitely too mature to be involving himself in stupid duels.

She wondered how someone who had been so brave in the war, and was clearly an intelligent man, had lowered himself to such childish antics.

'You are disappointed in me,' he said with the perception that always unnerved her. Mr Harrington had left the room to find some wine, though Catherine suspected it was because he was rather squeamish. Suddenly alone with Mr Oakley, she became more aware of the fact that he was naked from the waist up. His torso was that of a sportsman, lean and hard, with hardly an ounce of spare fat.

She made a point of looking only at the wound. To see the rest of his torso was far too disturbing.

'I am sure it is none of my business,' she answered calmly as she inserted the next suture.

'Damn it, Catherine, your prodding with that needle suggests otherwise. Could you try and be a little kinder?' He took a deep breath. 'I apologise, Miss Willoughby. I should not swear like that in front of you.'

'You should have heard the things Jimmy used to say,' she said, with a smile. 'Believe me when I say that I am unshockable.'

'Really? Be careful, Miss Willoughby. Another less honourable man might take that statement, coming from such innocent lips, as a challenge.'

'And would you fight a duel for me if he did?' The moment she had uttered it, she wished she had not done so. It was asking for something to which she had no right.

'I would kill him long before we

reached the dueling ground.'

She looked at him, startled by his savage tone, and for a moment was lost in his deep blue eyes.

'I thought you said you were unshockable,' he said in a husky voice.

'What happened to the other man?' she asked, turning her head, afraid that if she looked at him any longer, he would know exactly how she felt about him. 'He is not dead, is he?'

There was only a momentary pause before his reply. 'No, he's quite well.'

'So you lost the duel?'

'Make up your mind, Miss Willoughby,' he said, grinning. 'You are either disappointed with me for fighting the duel, or disappointed with me for losing. You cannot have it both ways.'

'I am simply glad that you lost only the duel and not your life. Especially for such a trivial reason.'

'You do not think Mrs Somerson's honour worth fighting for?'

'It seems to me that if a woman has to call on a man to defend her honour, she must have behaved in a way that brought it into question.'

'No wonder Jimmy called you Cat. Those claws are quite sharp, are they not? Well, I am glad. It shows you are not as different from other women as I had thought you were.'

She did not reply, but had the grace to feel ashamed of her cattiness. She hoped he would not realise it was down to her jealousy of Mrs Somerson.

'The wound should mend now,' she said, as she finished bandaging. 'I shall leave you and Mr Harrington to your wine.' As she spoke, the man in question returned to the room with the wine and three glasses.

'Are you sure you will not join us, Miss Willoughby?' said Mr Oakley in rather more tender tones. 'You look distinctly pale, and rather as if you are about to fall down.'

'I have told you, I am not the swooning kind.' She wished she was not the crying kind, either, because at that moment she was struggling hard with the emotions he evoked in her. The idea that he could have died filled her with horror. Not because it would leave her and Alyssa without a benefactor, but because to lose him would be a pain she could not bear.

'I have been ungrateful,' he said gently. 'Especially after you have made such a good job of patching me up. I thank you.'

Catherine bid goodnight and curtseyed to both men.

'Catherine . . . ' She had reached the door when he spoke her name. 'I would much rather that none of our guests knew about this.'

'I shall not say anything to anyone.'

'Well — you would be a rare woman indeed if you kept your knowledge of this incident completely to yourself.'

'I think,' she said, 'that despite all the time you have spent amongst women in society, Mr Oakley, you do not really know us at all.'

Catherine went back to her room, and after she had changed out of her bloodstained nightdress and burned it on the fire, had to shift Alyssa across the bed so that she had space to get back in.

'Where have you been, Cat?' her sister murmured.

'I went downstairs to get a drink, dearest. Go back to sleep.'

★　★　★

The following morning at the breakfast table, Catherine half expected the talk to be of the duel. She felt sure that Mr Oakley would tell Mrs Somerson how he had defended her honour, and that the lady would want everyone to know. Instead the talk was about the miraculous escape from France of one of Mr Oakley's friends.

'I heard from my valet, who heard from a friend who has come up from London this morning. Bertie Carter managed to get across the Channel, but it seems some of the blighters followed him over, and tried to attack him at a coaching inn,' one of the young men was saying in excited tones. 'Luckily the Captain turned up and saw them off. But imagine! Frenchies on British soil. They must have wanted Carter back badly.'

'Probably because his father is in the government,' Oakley suggested. 'They see the sons of noblemen and diplomats as perfect bargaining tools.'

'I have heard that Bertie might have had some secret information,' said the young man, widening his eyes for greater effect.

'I hardly think Bertie Carter is capable of such a mission.' Mr Oakley's tone was dismissive.

'I don't know. They say he is friends with the Captain.'

'Thank God for the Captain,' fluttered Mrs Somerson. 'They say he is very dashing and handsome. Oh, you must not be jealous, Xander, dear.' Mr Oakley had shown no signs of being so. 'You know how I feel about you.'

'Yes, but they say he was wounded,'

went on the young man. Most of the table were more interested in the story of Bertie Carter's escape than in Mrs Somerson's declarations of love. 'One of the Frenchies stuck him with his sword.'

'Do we have to have such bloodthirsty discussions at the breakfast table?' remarked Mr Oakley. 'It's quite enough to put a man's mind off his eggs.' As he spoke, Catherine tried to catch his eye, but he pointedly turned away from her to address Mrs Somerson.

Catherine dropped her hands into her lap, to hide the fact that they were trembling uncontrollably. Things that she had seen and heard out of context now took on new meaning. She remembered Mr Harrington saying that Mr Oakley had been 'busted down to Captain' for insubordination. How could she have been so stupid, not to recognise that Jimmy's adoration for Mr Oakley was very much the same as his adoration for the Captain?

It was not a matter of Mr Oakley and

the Captain as separate entities in her brother's life. It was the same hero worship — for the same brave and noble man.

5

As she struggled to regain composure, whilst the other guests chattered around her, part of Catherine's heart was terrified for Mr Oakley — whilst the other part was ridiculously happy that he had not been fighting some trivial duel, but had actually been defending his friend against the French. Bertie Carter, whoever he was, must have sent word that he was in trouble.

She had so many questions she wished to ask Mr Oakley, but she also understood he would not want to hear them. He had a view of women as being prattlers, and he would expect her to be the same. But she also wanted him to know that not only would she never betray him, but she might also be able to help him with his important work. Jimmy's death must have halted some of the Captain's activities if he had not yet found someone trustworthy to forge new documents for escapees.

She was brought out of her reverie by the conversation at the breakfast table, which had turned to the King and the fact that he was holding a parade before Easter.

'Will we be in London then?' asked Alyssa. 'I should love to see it.'

'Yes, I see no reason why we cannot leave a little earlier,' answered Oakley. 'In fact, Andrew and I must leave in the morning on Court business. I shall make sure my house in London is ready for your arrival in a few days.'

'You are leaving?' said Mrs Somerson, with her customary pout. 'But Xander, I have hardly seen you. Perhaps I should return to London.'

'Do not cut short your visit on my account,' said Mr Oakley. 'I shall be far too busy with His Majesty to entertain you all. Why not stay on here, and travel down with the Miss Willoughbys and my aunt on Wednesday?'

Mrs Somerson looked as if she had

rather do anything but. 'Whilst I am sure their company will be *delightful*' — she said it in the manner of someone who had been offered a dead cat — 'I too have things to take care of in London this week. Lord Granchester has invited me to dinner on Tuesday evening.' She gave Mr Oakley a look that was at once pathetic and comical.

'I am sure you will enjoy that greatly.' He put down his napkin and stood up. 'If you will excuse me, I am going riding. Does anyone wish to join me?'

As most of the guests were feeling the effects of the night before, they declined. Catherine was sorely tempted to ask if she could join him, so they could speak, but when she attempted once more to catch his eye, she felt sure that he pointedly ignored her and left the room.

She thought to go with him anyway, but before she could do so, Phoebe Somerson rose and followed him out, so she lost her chance.

'Xander . . . Xander, wait,' called Phoebe. 'You are being so mean to me.'

Oakley was already on his way out of the front door. 'Do not make a scene, Phoebe,' he said, in mild but firm tones. His groom was waiting with his horse, and he wasted no time in mounting it. He hoped that Phoebe was too self-absorbed to notice him wincing. His side still hurt, and he knew he probably should not be riding at all, but he was desperate to get away on his own for a while. He could see that Catherine wished to speak to him, but he could not deal with her until he had worked out a plan of action. He had seen the realisation dawn in her face when she heard about the Captain's injury. He had to find a way of putting her off that track, before she shared her idea with someone else.

'I am not making a scene,' protested Phoebe. 'No one else is here.' He had almost forgotten her presence. Clearly, to her, his groom did not count as a person, which annoyed him greatly.

'I expected you to come to me last night, and you did not,' Phoebe continued. The well-trained groom moved away, to the side of the house.

'And neither did I intend to. You must see the impropriety of such behaviour when I am responsible for two young girls living in my house.'

He was beginning to see that inviting Phoebe had been a bad idea. He had mistakenly thought she would take the girls under her wing and perhaps even help him with guiding them in society. Whilst she had made a fuss of Alyssa to begin with, she had soon grown bored of playing the big sister, and he could not help noticing that she had been particularly rude to Catherine from the outset.

This weekend was the longest he had spent in Phoebe's company. Before then, they had either met at functions in Court, surrounded by many others, and during the times they had been alone, they had done little in the way of talking. Familiarity had made her seem tiresome. Or perhaps — if he were more honest — comparison with Catherine had brought that about.

'Fatherhood has turned you into a bore,' complained Phoebe.

'I am their guardian, not their father.' Did she have to insist on reminding him of his age in relation to Catherine?

'Guardian, father, it matters little. You have become all moral and upstanding. You were more fun when you were not. I do have other beaux, you know. Men who would be more than happy to spend time with me.'

'I hope that one of them will make you happy, Phoebe.' He spoke as kindly as he could, but he had to let her know that their liaison was definitely over. 'I doubt very much that I could.'

'You are a brute!'

Xander rode away, wondering what on earth had got into Phoebe. They both knew how the game was played. When it was time to move on from a love affair, both parties were meant to leave with their dignity intact.

As he rode on, and the breeze cleared his head, he began to feel guilty. He *had* treated Phoebe badly. It was a mistake to bring her to Oakley Castle this weekend. It had given her the impression that he was planning to take their relationship further by making her his wife. He was sure she was not the only one who thought so.

He would have to do something to ease Phoebe's feelings of abandonment. A present, perhaps. A transaction to buy her off. Pulling the horse up a mile from Oakley Castle, pain seared his side and he wanted to cry out in anger and frustration. He had become the sort of man he was sure he had only pretended to be; a part of the hypocritical society he secretly despised. A dandy, who treated his lovers in a cavalier fashion, then paid them not to make a fuss when it was over.

He found himself wondering what Catherine would think of his behaviour.

Catherine. It all came back to her. Had she not disturbed his equilibrium, he might have found a kinder way to end his romance with Phoebe when the inevitable end came. From the moment he had spoken to Catherine in the study at Willoughby Manor, and seen her stick out her proud little chin, he realised he had not wanted any other woman in his life.

She had shown great courage in dealing with his injury, too, whereas most women of his acquaintance would have fainted on the spot, but that did not mean he could ask her to share the dangerous world he inhabited. His instinct was to protect her and keep her from harm.

Perhaps he should marry Phoebe. She would be as good a wife as any, if he could not have the woman he truly loved. But the idea of a marriage which would surely end with both of them taking other lovers disgusted him. He had to get away. To escape.

Perhaps it was time for another trip

to France. Except that it would mean leaving Catherine. It was the right thing to do, to keep her out of it altogether — but that did not mean he felt happy about leaving her.

Recklessly he spurred on his horse, deciding to spend the day checking the far reaches of his estate. He had neglected it lately, with so many other events unfolding. It would give him an excuse not to return to Oakley Castle and Phoebe's resentment until the evening.

★ ★ ★

Mrs Somerson had no compunction about letting all the guests at Oakley Castle know she was in a foul mood. Mid-morning, one of the maids, Kitty, dropped a tray she was carrying when Mrs Somerson careered into her.

'You stupid creature!' cried Mrs Somerson, striking out at Kitty and clipping her around the ear. 'If it were up to me, you'd lose your post.'

It was a very unladylike way to behave, thought Catherine, and she could see the other guests were embarrassed. But no one stepped forward to speak up for Kitty.

In the face of everyone's seeming indifference, though she accepted it was probably more down to embarrassment, Catherine instinctively got up to help the girl pick up the mess.

'No, Miss Willoughby, you should not do this,' said Kitty, with tears in her eyes. The poor girl was trembling with terror. 'I'm ever so sorry.'

'Do not be. You have done nothing wrong. Griffiths — ' Catherine beckoned the butler over. 'Perhaps someone else could clean up this mess? I believe Kitty needs a break.'

'I'll see to it she has a cup of tea in the scullery, Miss Willoughby,' said Griffiths, bowing and smiling warmly at Catherine. 'And I shall send one of the other maids to clean up.'

'Thank you. I shall come along and speak to you later, Kitty. No, do not look so worried. You are not in trouble.'

Catherine waited until Kitty had been escorted away before turning on Mrs Somerson. She knew she should try to be calm and civilised, but her emotions ran away with her. 'You had no right to hit that girl.'

'I had every right. She is a clumsy fool. Mr Harrington!' she appealed to that gentleman. 'The child is an imbecile, is she not?'

It was unclear whether Mrs Somerson was referring to Kitty or Catherine. Harrington stammered, clearly not wanting to be drawn in to the argument.

'When I am mistress here, there will be changes,' Phoebe snapped.

'But as you are not the mistress yet, I think you might at least treat Mr Oakley's staff with civility,' said Catherine in a firm, quiet voice that belied the pain she felt in her heart. She knew then that she had to get away somehow. If what Mrs Somerson said was true, and she was going to be mistress at Oakley Castle, then Catherine could not bear to live there and see her with Mr Oakley every day.

'I shall also tell him to reconsider his regrettable habit of taking in penniless waifs,' spat Phoebe, before holding her head high and starting to walk up the stairs. She turned back with a parting shot. 'But as I am not an unkind person, I am sure I could persuade him to keep you on as a maid, since you are so obviously at home in that sort of company.'

'How dare you — ' Alyssa started to say in defence of her sister, only to be stopped by Mr Harrington's hand on her arm.

'Let her go, dearest,' he said in a low voice. 'I believe she has lost a battle, and this is one last rally before she admits defeat.'

Catherine longed to ask him what he meant but, aware that — in the lady's absence — all eyes were now on her, she felt a sudden need to escape. She murmured an apology for her behaviour and curtseyed politely to the other guests, before excusing herself and retreating to hide in the castle library until lunchtime.

When Mr Oakley did not appear at lunch or during the afternoon, Catherine began to fear she might never get a chance to speak to him. After lunch, she kept her promise and went to speak to the maid.

'Are you recovered now, Kitty?' she asked, taking a seat at the kitchen table. Kitty's cheek still bore a red mark.

'Yes, Miss Willoughby, I thank you, I am much better. I'm not in any trouble, am I? Mr Griffiths said I'm not, but . . . '

'I'm sure Mr Oakley will be very upset to know what happened. But he will not be angry with you — and if he is, I shall tell him that he has no right to be. I cannot imagine he is ever unkind to his servants.'

'Oh no, Miss Willoughby, you are right. The master is ever so kind. And very handsome.' Kitty blushed. 'I mean . . . he's a proper gentleman.'

Catherine smiled. 'I know what you mean.'

'Do you think he's going to marry Mrs Somerson? Oh, I shouldn't ask. It's none of my business, but . . . all the servants are worried.'

'I do not know, Kitty. But if he does, I shall speak to him and obtain his assurance that you will all still be treated well.'

'Thank you, Miss Willoughby. We have liked having you and Miss Alyssa here. Mr Griffiths said it's nice to have pretty young ladies living at Oakley Castle again. But he thinks Mrs Somerson is going to send you away.'

'We would probably have to go away one day anyway, Kitty. My sister may marry, and when she does, I shall probably go and live with her.'

'You might marry as well, Miss Willoughby.'

'No. I . . . I do not think I will.'

'Sometimes it is hard, when you love a person so much, to think of loving someone else,' murmured Kitty, with a perception that surprised Catherine. 'But you are so beautiful.' She dropped her eyes to the floor. 'I'm sorry, I always speak out of turn. Mr Griffiths tells me off about it all the time. He says I will never make a ladies' maid if I do not learn to be quiet.'

'Is that what you wish to be?'

'Oh yes, Miss Willoughby. I should love it.'

'Very well — I need a maid for when I go to London. I have been sharing Jenny with Miss Alyssa.' Catherine did not tell Kitty that was because she was trying to limit the amount of money Mr Oakley spent on her. 'But it is a great deal of work for one girl, especially as we shall be attending lots of balls and coming home late. If you would like the post as my maid . . . '

'Oh, Miss Willoughby, that's so kind of you. I would love it. I shall look after you ever so well.'

'I know you will, Kitty. Get a good night's sleep tonight, then start in the morning. I shall let Mr Griffiths know about your change of employment.'

'Will Mr Oakley mind?'

'Leave that to me. He has said that I should have my own maid, so he cannot very well refuse.'

Catherine secretly hoped the arrangement might keep the girl out of Mrs Somerson's orbit, and that she might be able to take her with her when she left. Catherine liked Kitty. She was open, honest and eager to do well.

★   ★   ★

All the guests started to worry when Mr Oakley also missed dinner. Apart from Mrs Somerson, who drank heavily and flirted outrageously with all the young men. But it was clear from their eyes that she had lost some of her allure. They made the right replies, but to Catherine — although she might have imagined it — their compliments seemed half-hearted.

Mr Harrington did not even bother to pretend. He spent the whole evening talking to Alyssa. One of the young men, realising that Catherine was without attention, did his best to amuse her, but gave up when it became clear that her mind was on other things.

'I believe the master has encountered some problems on the estate,' Griffiths informed Mr Harrington when he asked after Mr Oakley. 'He sent a message asking that the cook leave a cold platter for him.'

When it became clear that Mr Oakley was not going to return until very late, Catherine had no choice but to go up to bed when the others did so. Griffiths stopped her just as she was about to go upstairs.

'Miss Willoughby, I wished you to know that I have prepared Kitty for her new post as your maid.'

'That is very kind. Thank you, Griffiths.'

'You can trust Kitty, Miss Willoughby. She is a good girl. Prattles a little much for my liking, but there is no harm in her. In truth, you may trust all the servants at Oakley Castle. All of us are happy to serve you and Miss Alyssa in any way we can. Nothing will change that.'

Catherine sensed he was not being unctuous. He was letting her know something very important in the event that Mrs Somerson married Mr Oakley. She and Alyssa would not be without friends.

'Thank you, Griffiths. I hope I have not caused you problems by taking one of the housemaids.'

'If I may be so bold as to say it, some people are worth going to a little extra trouble over, Miss Willoughby.' Griffiths bowed to her, and then went about his business.

When Alyssa came to Catherine's room later that night, it was not with her usual buoyancy. She looked troubled. She climbed into the bed and pulled the covers over her head, something she had done since she was little, and it reminded Catherine that in many ways, her sister was still a child.

'What is it, dearest?' Catherine had

already guessed the answer. She pulled the covers from Alyssa's head.

'I've tried so hard not to love Mr Harrington, Cat. Really I have. But no other man is like him. I cannot bear the thought of being with someone else — even if he is rich and can buy me pretty dresses.'

'Sometimes your heart wants what it wants, darling.' Catherine stroked Alyssa's fair curls.

'But he does not think Mr Oakley will give his permission, because Andrew is broke, like we are.'

'Would you like me to speak to Mr Oakley?'

'Would you?' Alyssa sat up, her glum expression dissipating in moments. 'But I thought you wanted me to marry someone rich, Cat.'

'I wanted you to marry someone who could take care of you, and whether Mr Harrington has money or not, I have no doubt he will do that.'

Catherine knew what Alyssa did not. Harrington was one of the Captain's men, and therefore just as brave and noble as Mr Oakley. She had no doubt that he would guard Alyssa with his life.

She was also realistic enough to know that an upper-class man's idea of being broke was not the same as the poverty to be found in the darkest parts of England. It merely meant one could not afford horses or expensive balls, nor to have an army of servants. Even when the Willoughbys' fortunes were at their lowest ebb, they somehow managed to put food on the table. Only Jimmy's death, and his annuity dying with him, had left Catherine and Alyssa in dire straits.

Whether Alyssa would understand that, when she wanted pretty dresses that Harrington could not provide, was another matter. But that she loved him was unquestionable, and Catherine realised that she did not want her sister to be subjected to a loveless society marriage, any more than she wanted one for herself.

'But I won't be able to look after you as I wanted to,' said Alyssa, breaking into Catherine's reverie.

'Forget me, and think of being happy. I am sure Mr Oakley would not allow me to starve.'

Catherine spoke with a certainty she did not feel. Once she confessed all to him, he might well do just that. She was wise enough to know that men could forgive sins in other men that they would not accept in a woman.

She lay awake whilst Alyssa slept, waiting for the sound of Mr Oakley returning. When she heard hooves on the ground outside, she dressed quickly and went downstairs, bracing herself for the battle ahead.

6

She found the master of the house in his study, sitting behind his desk in the dim candlelight. In front of him was a platter of food he had not touched, and a glass of brandy.

'I hear you have a new maid,' he said, gesturing to a seat opposite him.

'Erm . . . yes, I thought Kitty would be a good maid and I need one for London and . . . ' She was tempted to tell him about Mrs Somerson, but her feelings for him prevented her. She was forced to admit that she might not have entirely pure reasons for lowering Phoebe in his estimation. 'I hope that arrangement is acceptable to you.'

'Nothing happens in Oakley Castle without my learning of it,' he replied. 'I'm aware of the . . . *scene* . . . today. Griffiths was quite emphatic that nothing like that ever happens to one of the servants again. I quite agree with him that Mrs Somerson's behaviour was scandalous. You have my assurance that neither Kitty, the staff here, or staff in any of my other houses will be subjected to such treatment again.'

Was he telling her that he had no intentions of marrying Mrs Somerson? Her heart felt lighter briefly, but then she wondered whether he just planned to extract a promise from the lady that she would not abuse the servants.

'Thank you. But that is not why I came to speak to you.'

'Is this where you tell me how you have unearthed my brilliant disguise?' he said, sardonically. 'Because I can assure you that there is a young man in London more than happy to swear that I dueled with him last night.'

'No, it is not about the Captain. At least, not yet. It concerns Alyssa and Mr Harrington.'

'Yes, I am aware of their feelings for each other. I would have to be blind not to be. But you are the one who wished your sister to marry a rich man.'

'Only so that she would be properly cared for. But I am sure that Harrington will take care of her.'

'He is broke.' He spoke bluntly.

'Only in relative terms, I am sure.'

'I am sorry, but my duty is to ensure both you and your sister marry well. As your legal guardian, I cannot give my permission to Andrew and Alyssa, as much as I, too, would be happy to see them marry.'

'About that . . . '

'What?' He met her eyes.

'This is where we start talking about the Captain.'

'Blackmail will not work, Catherine. I have already told you that there is a young man in London willing to swear we duelled last night.'

'No, I am not trying to blackmail you. I am merely attempting to release you from your promise.'

'Explain.' His eyes pierced her, but there was something else in them. A wariness. 'On second thoughts — do not. There may be some things it is better I do not know.'

'I have to tell you. If only because I misjudged you. I thought you were a dandy — someone only devoted to pleasure. And I was wrong.'

'What has this got to do with my being your guardian?'

'Everything. But I have to go back to the beginning. To when Jimmy used to get notes from Father, excusing him from lessons at school.'

'There are some things I do not need to know.' Mr Oakley spoke sternly. 'Go back to bed, Catherine.'

'No. You have to listen to me. When I told you I did not know the false names of the people who killed Jimmy, I lied.'

'What were their names?' His question was like a pistol shot.

'The names that were on the forged documents were Annette and Paulette Du Pont.'

'Women? What type of documents were they? This is very important.'

'They were letters of introduction.'

'For France?'

She shook her head. 'No, for passage to America. The letters stated that the two women were of impeccable character and had escaped from the guillotine, and that they were to be given safe passage to America. It promised that the costs would be met by the writer of the letters. The signature on them was that of a French nobleman.' She named the nobleman in question.

Mr Oakley rose and began pacing the room. 'I know the man. He is an exile here in England, and he has done a similar service to those escaping from the revolution in the past, so it would raise no eyebrows. He has a very strict procedure for helping people, which is probably why they needed the forgeries. I imagine that by the time the accounts are put before him, the women will be well on their way to America, if not there already. But why would they need false names?'

'I do not know, but they assured Jimmy that it was for a noble cause,'

Catherine said, fearing his anger. 'He told me just before he died — when I was worried about it — that the request for the letters came from an impeccable source.'

'I cannot understand why Jimmy would be so trusting. He was always so careful. So it must be someone whom we know. Someone who seemed beyond reproach in his eyes. Thank you for telling me.' He stretched and grimaced. 'Now I want you to go to bed and put all this out of your mind.'

'I have not finished yet.'

'You have more information?'

'Not exactly. I just need to tell you something. Jimmy was not the forger.'

'Think carefully before you speak, Catherine . . . '

'I must tell you. It was not Jimmy who wrote those notes to get out of lessons; it was me. And it was not Jimmy who forged documents for the Captain; it was me. Jimmy has never been good at art. In fact, he barely wrote anything unless he had to. He realised when I was twelve that I had a talent for copying artists, and at first we just did it as a joke.'

'I do not want to know about any of this.' Despite his words, Catherine guessed that he had known, if not from the beginning, then for some time. 'In fact, I refuse to believe it. A woman could not possibly be capable of such subterfuge.'

'Why? Because we are all sweet, helpless little things who wouldn't so much as strike a servant?'

'Go to bed, Catherine.'

'I have not yet finished.'

'Dear Lord, woman, do you intend to keep me up all night? I thought you were not a prattler.'

'I told you that I misjudged you.'

'Oh, well, then I accept your apology.' He waved his hand dismissively. 'There is no need to discuss this any further.'

'So when Jimmy died I was angry with you, because if he had not wanted to buy a horse to ride in your steeplechase, he would not have taken on the new work. So I . . . it was not Jimmy who wrote asking you to be our guardian. It was me.'

'You forged that document too? Well, you are a real mistress of the art.'

'I wanted to be sure Alyssa was cared for. But now I know you. Now I know how kind, brave and noble you are, I wish to deceive you no longer. So I absolve you of your promise. Alyssa can marry Harrington, and I can . . . '

'What? Become a forger?'

'I thought that perhaps the Captain, who has always been happy with my work in the past, might . . . '

'Over my dead body! You will never forge anything again, Catherine. Do you hear me?'

'But you are not my guardian.' Catherine stood up, determined to make her point. 'You cannot tell me what to do!'

'On the contrary, I have a letter from your brother that says otherwise, and whether or not I have a legal obligation,

I still consider that I have a moral obligation to care for you and Alyssa.'

'But I have told you. It is a fake.'

'Shall we test that with the magistrate?'

'I would be sent to prison . . . hanged.' Catherine felt her knees tremble. 'I know what you are trying to do, and it is wonderful of you — '

'Please.' He held up his hand to stop her. 'Do not get any romantic notions about why I am doing this. I should throw you in the gutter, but I do not believe your sister, who I am sure is innocent of this crime, should suffer for your actions. So I will continue with my task of introducing you both to society, and hope to God that I find you a husband who does not discover the truth about your past.'

Catherine's hands flew to her face in horror as tears started to fall. She had expected him to be angry, and justifiably so — but not this. After all, had she not helped him when he was the Captain? And had he not been grateful for that help when he believed it came from Jimmy? But, of course, there were the double standards she had considered before. She just had not expected to be faced with the hypocrisy quite so brutally.

He stepped forward with his arm stretched out, and for a horrible moment she thought he might strike her. She shrank back. 'I only did it for Alyssa,' she whispered. 'That is why I wanted no dresses or anything for myself.'

'I — er . . . ' Mr Oakley's voice sounded constricted, and his hand fell to his side. 'I will give Alyssa until the end of the Season, just to be sure she does not fall in love with the next young man who tells her she is beautiful. You — er . . . you must realise that is a possibility, and it is only right that we wait. If by that time she is still in love with Harrington, and he with her, I shall settle enough money on her so that they might at least live in comfort.'

'Thank you.' Catherine turned and

fled, hardly noticing as she stumbled up the stairs that Mrs Somerson's maid was lurking in a corner.

★ ★ ★

'You were a bit harsh on Miss Willoughby, old man,' said Harrington as he and Xander travelled by phaeton to London the following morning. 'In fact, if I had been there I might have called you out. If not for her expertise, the Captain and his band may have been arrested by the French long ago.'

Though Xander did not like to talk about his private feelings, the events of the night before disturbed him so much he had told Andrew some of what had happened. He could still see Catherine's stricken expression as he had insulted her. He had reached out his hand to comfort her, ashamed with himself for hurting her, only to see her shrink back, as if she thought him about to hit her. It left a deep shame burning within him.

But he told himself it was for the best. He had, hopefully, killed two birds with one stone. She could not possibly hero-worship him now. Not after he had been so unkind. The thought was like a sword piercing his heart, but he kept telling himself it was for the best.

He sighed heavily. 'I know, Andrew. I would have probably let you win the duel. But do you not see that I had to make sure she never does it again?' His lips were set in a grim line as he explained the other reason for his harshness. 'Whether Jimmy wrote that letter about guardianship or not, I owe it to him to protect her. Damn it, Andrew, if she is the one who has been helping us these past two years, I owe it to *her*. Jimmy was fooled by someone telling him that they had a noble cause, and he had been taught to be very careful. Who knows what danger she might get herself into if she tried to make her living in such a way? She has no idea who to trust, and as a woman in this difficult world, she is even more vulnerable than Jimmy was. I had to let her believe it was reprehensible.'

'Thank God the crooks who wanted the forged documents are not aware that she knows the names, or that she is the one who did the forgeries,' commented Andrew.

'It does not bear thinking about. It cost him his life, but at least Jimmy protected her up to the end.'

'Do you really think they might be something to do with the intelligence from France? About the attempt on the king's life?'

Xander nodded. 'I am sure of it. The trouble is finding them before the day. It might be too late once they are in amongst the crowd.'

'Did you ever suspect it might not be Jimmy doing the forgeries?'

'Not at first. Then I saw Miss Willoughby's painting; she is accomplished. Very accomplished. It also reminded me that I had never seen Jimmy so much as doodle. I did not know about the guardianship letter, though I ought to have suspected, as it came at the same time as the news of his death.'

'Are you really angry with her about that?'

'No.' Xander smiled. 'It was a very sensible and clever thing to do. And as I have said, I do have a moral obligation to help Jimmy's family. Just as I have the same obligation to see you and Alyssa happy.'

'Thank you for that.'

'You realise you might lose her, Andrew. She is still very young.'

'I know. I am prepared for that: Or at least, that is what I keep telling myself. What about you, Xander?'

'What about me?' Xander stiffened.

'You are not going to marry Phoebe, are you?'

'No! Even if she had not struck Kitty, I had already made up my mind that Phoebe was not meant to be Mrs Oakley.'

'Do you have anyone else in mind?'

'No. No one at all.' Xander urged the

horses on, speeding up the phaeton and making it clear that the subject was closed.

★   ★   ★

'Is it true?' Alyssa danced around Catherine's bedroom as sunlight streamed through the windows. 'Did Mr Oakley really say that?'

'Yes.' Catherine forced a smile, wanting to be happy for her sister. 'You just have to promise me you will not fall in love with someone else with no money. I do not think he would be as generous for anyone but Harrington.'

'I shall never love anyone else. And if Mr Oakley settles enough money on me, then you can come and live with us.' Alyssa grabbed Catherine around the waist and spun her around.

'I think . . . I think I may find somewhere else to live,' said Catherine.

'Why? Don't you want to be with me?'

'Of course I do, but I have a feeling

you and Harrington will prefer to be alone.' The truth, which Catherine did not wish to admit to Alyssa, was that Mr Oakley would probably be a regular guest at their home, and Catherine knew beyond a doubt that she had to go where she never had to see him again. Her love for him was too deep, and the pain his angry words had caused was too raw. She only hoped she could get through the Season and Alyssa and Andrew's wedding without making a fool of herself in his company. Fortunately it was unlikely that she would have to be alone with him. Or that he would even want to be alone with her — which caused her even more pain, even as she acknowledged that it was for the best.

'What's happened, darling?' asked Alyssa. 'I know you are unhappy.'

'I'm not. I am very happy for you.'

'You think I don't notice things, but I do. I have seen the way you look at Mr Oakley.' Alyssa caressed her sister's cheek.

'Please, Alyssa, do not ask me anything. I cannot . . . I cannot . . . ' Catherine was saved by Kitty knocking the door and entering the room.

'I am sorry to interrupt, Miss Willoughby, I just brought back your gown. I have darned the hem and 'tis as good as new.'

'Thank you, Kitty. Will you put it away?'

'Yes, Miss Willoughby.' Kitty looked excited about something.

'What has happened?' Catherine asked her.

'Oh, Miss Willoughby, I shouldn't gossip, I know, but there's been all sorts going on this morning. Mrs Somerson has left. Mr Griffiths says good riddance to bad rubbish, which I know he shouldn't, but . . . Anyway, she caused such a fuss, screaming and shouting at everyone that she wouldn't set foot in this . . . I can't say the word she used then, it's blasphemous . . . place again. Then, would you believe her maid, Celine, steps forward and slaps her on the face?

Then Celine says, 'You've ruined every-thing'.'

'What?' Catherine and Alyssa spoke together. That a servant should behave in such a way to her mistress was incomprehensible.

'I know, we could not believe it either, but Griffiths was in the hall and saw it with his own eyes. Then when Mrs Somerson had gone, Mr Oakley told Griffiths that she was not to appear on any of his guest lists ever again.'

'Did Mrs Somerson dismiss her maid?' asked Alyssa.

'No, Miss Alyssa. She actually said sorry to her for being so hysterical, Griffiths said. It was so funny.' Kitty laughed, and then remembered who she was with. 'Not as I'd ever slap one of my ladies. And Mr Oakley comes to me, when I was in the servants' hall eating my breakfast, and said in such a kind voice. 'I'm very sorry for what happened yesterday, Kitty and that I wasn't here to deal with it at the time. I know you will be well-treated as Miss

Willoughby's maid'. He didn't have to do that at all, did he? He's such a nice gentleman.' Kitty's face took on a dreamy expression, suggesting that she had her own fantasies about Mr Oakley. 'Let's hope he finds himself a real lady to marry now. Not that I should be saying such things. Sorry, Miss Willoughby, Miss Alyssa.'

'Don't worry, Kitty. I hope so, too,' said Catherine gently.

Kitty had gone when Alyssa turned to Catherine and after giving her a lingering look, breathed, 'Oh, dearest . . . '

Catherine took her sister's hand. 'Help me, Alyssa, to get through the next few months.'

'Of course I will, darling. Wait until we get to London. There will be so many handsome men wanting to dance with you, you'll soon forget him.'

Catherine doubted that very much, but she nodded and quipped, 'I shall be the belle of the ball. Or at least the belle of any ball that you don't attend.'

7

Mr Oakley's London mansion was every bit as luxurious as Oakley Castle. Situated in Kensington, it was perfectly placed for the many entertainments London had to offer. On Catherine and Alyssa's first night in the Capital, he had arranged a ball, to which a hundred people were invited.

'Is it not wonderful, Catherine?' asked Alyssa as they walked to the ballroom. Alyssa was dressed in a pure white tulle gown, with a sprig of snowdrops in her hair, looking the epitome of spring. Catherine had chosen a dress of green satin, and had piled her dark hair high on her head.

'It is very exciting,' said Catherine. She could not deny that the setting was thrilling, even if she had convinced herself she would hate being in London. The room was a symphony of colour, as men and women vied to wear the brightest outfits. Mr Oakley wore a jacket of dark red, with an intricate but subtle gold pattern. Despite the relative plainness of his attire, Catherine could not help thinking that he stood out from all the other men.

Alyssa was naturally a sensation, but Catherine also drew her fair share of admirers, as young men queued up to dance with her. At one point she looked across and saw Mr Oakley dancing with her sister, and hoped that she might be asked next. They had barely spoken since she arrived in London with Alyssa, and then only to exchange the usual pleasantries.

As the evening wore on, it became clear he was not going to ask her to dance. She tried not to let it matter; as she smiled and chatted with the men who were interested in her whilst barely remembering their names. The triviality of it all only increased her feelings of disassociation. Her heart grew heavier, and she wondered how she was ever going to survive the Season.

When the heat in the room became too much, she used it as an excuse to escape to the garden and get her breath back. Whilst there was still some frost in the mornings, the weather had become milder as spring arrived.

Oakley Mansion, whilst not boasting grounds as extensive as Oakley Castle, had a pretty garden, where daffodils and snowdrops covered the flowerbeds. Catherine walked the narrow paths, taking deep breaths and trying to calm her fevered brow.

'Do you tire of your admirers already?'

Catherine turned to see Oakley following her. Now she was alone with him, she wished he would go away. She was afraid he might be unkind to her again, and she did not have the strength to argue back.

'I am not used to so much dancing. And I rather think they were Alyssa's admirers, who were only dancing with me until she was available.'

'You are too modest. I have already

had two young men approach me declaring undying love for you, and asking for your hand.'

'I have hardly said two words to the majority of the men who asked me to dance. I hope you told them I was not in the market for a husband.'

He snorted. 'I would never be foolish enough to make such a blanket statement, even if you are.'

'Oh yes, I forget. Your plan is to unload me and my nefarious behaviour as soon as possible.'

'Now you are being childish. The two young men who asked are from good families, and would be able to offer you a good life.'

'I do not want this sort of life,' declared Catherine. 'Where husbands and wives are frowned upon for spending time together, and each find a lover as soon as a respectable amount of time has passed. I may have done something that you believe is reprehensible, but I have not yet had to sell myself in order to eat.'

'You were quite content to sell your sister.'

Enraged, Catherine raised her hand to slap him, but he caught it before she reached his face and spoke with intensity. 'Do not ever try to strike me again, Catherine. I do not believe in hitting women, but I also believe it cuts both ways. A lady should never strike a man, either.'

'I hate you!'

'Really?' At that he pulled her into his arms and kissed her.

She wanted to pull away. She should have stopped him, but being in his arms and feeling his hungry mouth on hers was everything she had ever wanted. She let herself fall into the kiss, forgetting propriety and any idea that she was supposed to hate him, as fire coursed through her body.

Just as quickly as he had seized her, he set her away from him. 'I apologise,' he said abruptly. 'I should not have done that.'

'Xander . . . ' she whispered softly.

'I shall speak to the young men who approached me, and let you know their names. I trust you will take at least one of the offers seriously.'

'You want me to marry someone else? After that kiss?'

'I think the sooner you are married, the better.'

'Yes,' said Catherine, struggling to restrain her temper. 'You are right. I am a danger to myself if I allow one kiss to convince me that a man cares for me. Since you are obviously so wise and all-knowing, why don't you choose my husband from the likely contenders? I will abide by your decision. Just tell me where to be on my wedding day.' She was gratified to see that he looked as shocked as if she had indeed slapped him.

★ ★ ★

Catherine had never felt so homesick. She had almost succeeded in convincing herself that Willoughby Manor was no longer her home. But the morning after the ball, after a sleepless and distressful night, she wished she was there, in her old room overlooking the park. They had had nothing, but it made life much less complicated.

She had some money left over from the funds Mr Oakley had given her for the dressmaker, having only bought what was necessary, despite his insistence she buy an entire wardrobe. She guessed that, like most men, he would not really notice what she wore, or whether she was seen in the same dress twice. It was the sort of thing only other women noticed. He could probably get his money back for most of them. She would have no need for such gowns in the country.

The question was whether Cousin George would be willing to take her in. She would have to throw herself on his mercy and make him see that he could not abandon her. Anything would be better than Mr Oakley choosing a husband for her, and having to spend her life with a man she could never love as she loved him!

She thought of writing to Cousin George first, but decided the urgency of the situation might have more impact if she appeared on the doorstep.

As it was early, and the ball had finished extremely late, everyone else in the house had slept in. But if Catherine was to escape Aunt Harriet, she would have to be quick. She dressed in a dark blue travelling coat and a matching bonnet. She wrote a quick note to Alyssa, and with just a few items in a bag, she left the house long before Kitty was meant to wake her.

London in the morning was fascinating to see, before all the hustle and bustle began. Apart from some young urchins, there were few people around. She began to wish she could spend more time in the Capital; she and Alyssa had meant to go sightseeing with Aunt Harriet. She felt a pang as she thought of how she had left Alyssa behind. But her sister's happiness was assured. Catherine had no doubt that the love Alyssa and Harrington shared would last beyond the Season. Whilst Alyssa had been surrounded by doting young men the night before, her eyes had constantly scoured the room for Harrington. She had looked apprehensive until she had located him in the crowd, and then her frown had quickly turned to a smile.

As far as Catherine was concerned, she had done her best for her sister. She could do no more. If she did feel a pang of guilt at leaving Alyssa, the memory of Xander's kiss and his cruel words afterwards spurred her on through the early morning streets. Had her mind not been in such turmoil, she would have considered that there would be no welcome for her from Cousin George, and she might even have to retrace her steps, having no-one else to protect her. But she was committed to the course upon which she had set, and nothing would change her mind.

She headed towards a coaching

company, hoping she would be able to find one going north towards Willoughby Manor. As she walked, she became aware of a black closed-in carriage moving slowly behind her.

'Miss Willoughby!' a familiar voice said. 'It is Miss Willoughby, isn't it?'

She turned around to see Mrs Somerson leaning out of the window. 'Good morning,' said Catherine, in polite but icy tones. The carriage stopped alongside her, and she saw that it had two rather burly-looking men sitting at the front.

'Where are you headed on this fine morning? May I offer you a lift?'

Something made the back of Catherine's neck tingle. A feeling that all was not right. Mrs Somerson was being polite to her, for a start. That the lady was awake at such an early hour was another concern.

'Thank you,' she answered. 'But I had rather walk. I need the exercise.'

'Oh but it is much nicer to see London in a carriage, I always think. Please, do come and join me. I feel I owe you an apology for my behaviour at Oakley Castle.'

'I think Kitty is the one in need of an apology,' returned Catherine.

'Yes, that is why I wish to speak to you. Mr Oakley is furious with me. And justifiably so. I behaved badly. I was heartbroken you see, because . . . well, there are things I am sure he would rather I did not discuss with his ward. I had hoped that you might convince him that I see the error of my ways and wish to seek his forgiveness.'

'I do not wish to become involved,' answered Catherine. 'Besides, I am going away. I shall not be seeing him for some time.' As soon as the words were out, Catherine knew she had made a grave mistake. The two men, as if by some silent design, jumped down from the carriage and grabbed her. Before she could scream, one clamped his dirty hand over her mouth, whilst the other put a sack over her head. She struggled violently, but they were too strong for her.

'Quickly!' a woman's voice said. It was not Mrs Somerson's, and in her panic, Catherine could not place the speaker. 'Get her in the carriage.'

She was thrown roughly into the carriage and pinned in place, struggling to break free. 'Be quiet, you stupid girl!' came another voice. Someone clouted her hard around the head, and she fell into blackness.

★　★　★

Catherine did not know how long she was unconscious, only that when she came to, the sounds outside seemed to have changed. The city of London, even in the morning, had its own particular rhythm. But Catherine was a country girl, and it did not take her long to realise they had travelled into the countryside. She put her hand to her aching head and realised that, some-where along the way, she had lost her blue bonnet.

'Are you going to be sensible?' the

unknown woman asked her. 'If not, we will have to kill you.'

'Yes, I am.'

She felt the sacking being pulled from her, and struggled for a moment to focus. She found that she was sitting between Phoebe Somerson, and the French maid, Celine.

It was Celine's voice she had heard, but with a lower-class English accent. She seemed to be very much in control of the situation.

'So Mr Oakley believes you are going away?' jeered Celine. 'It is no good trying to lie. We've already heard you say it.'

'Yes. I left a note saying that I was travelling North to my old home. But they are sure to find out I have not reached my destination.'

'Willoughby Manor is a full day's travel from London,' said Celine, who was clearly very well-informed. 'It will take you a day to get there, and even if they write to you, it will not be soon, I think. Not when you have only just left.

So that's at least another day for the letter to reach Willoughby, and another day for your cousin — George, isn't it? — to write back and say you did not arrive. By then, it will all be over.'

Catherine did not wish to admit that no one might write to her at all, apart from Alyssa, and even she might wait a week or so. Mr Oakley would be glad to see the back of her, and she felt sure no one else who would miss her absence. 'What will be over?' she asked.

'Our task. The one you are going to help us with. Since you made it impossible for us to continue.'

'What do you mean?'

'You told Mr Oakley the names on the forged letters of introduction. Now they are unusable, so you have to create more.'

'I do not know what you are talking about.' Catherine's mind was working overtime. Celine had clearly been listening at the study door. Had she also picked up on Xander being the Captain? She prayed that was not the case.

Neither of them had said he was. Though there had been hints.

'Do not play innocent with me. We know it was you who forged the documents.'

'It was my brother, Jimmy and he is dead. I suppose it was your men who killed him.'

'They will kill you if you do not cooperate.'

'So be it. Even if I was able to do it, I had rather die than help you.'

'Then when you are dead, we will return to London and kill your sister.'

'Don't you dare hurt Alyssa!'

Celine gripped Catherine's arm. 'Then you had better do as we say.'

Catherine struggled for a moment, thinking she might jump out, but the carriage was going too fast. She did not fear death, if that was what awaited her, but she did fear it happening painfully over a long period of time as she lay with broken limbs in a ditch somewhere in the countryside.

She knew they were going to kill her

anyway. That much was certain. They could not afford to let her live once they had forced her to complete the task they set her. Just as they had killed Jimmy to silence him. But she could not let them hurt Alyssa. Her sister was an innocent in all of this. Although she knew about Catherine being involved in the forgery, she knew nothing of the details. What Xander had said about Alyssa suffering for her behaviour was coming true — but she had not thought for a moment that such a thing would happen.

'It was you who approached Jimmy, was it not?' Catherine asked, looking at Mrs Somerson. She wanted to get as much information as she could, in case she did manage to escape.

'He was one of my easier conquests. Unlike Mr Oakley. Even when Oakley was in my arms, I never felt that I really owned him.'

Catherine winced inwardly. She hated to think of Xander being with the Somerson woman — perhaps kissing her as he had kissed Catherine in the garden the night before.

'I feel sure Oakley knows who the Captain is,' said the maid. 'Has he said anything to you, Miss Willoughby?' Her voice was menacing.

'No.' Catherine shook her head.

'You must know who he is.'

'No, I don't.'

'I think you are lying. He used to visit your house. Are you telling me that you provided him with all those forged documents without ever knowing who he really was?'

'I did not provide him with anything. I do not know who he is. My brother never told me. The Captain was always in disguise and I only saw him from a distance. All I know is that he has a distinctly common accent.' She looked at Celine. 'Like yours.'

'Don't get impudent, Miss Willoughby. I might be tempted to kill you immediately, since you are apparently no use to us now. But I think you are.'

Blood ran through Catherine's veins

like iced water. She had never been so alone. Not only might she not live to see Alyssa marry, she was never going to see Xander again. And she wanted to see him, more than anything, just long enough to tell him how she felt. He might throw it back in her face, as he had the kiss, but at least he would know that she died loving him.

★   ★   ★

Catherine would have been surprised by how much Xander did notice. He had also spent a restless night, his own mind in turmoil about what had happened in the garden. He had behaved outrageously with an innocent young girl; what was more, to one he now acknowledged that he loved beyond measure. He vowed to put things right. He would beg her forgiveness and ask her to marry him. She might refuse, and he could hardly blame her if she did, but he hoped that once he had told her the depth of his feelings, she might look more kindly upon him. Not that he deserved her kindness. But if she let him, he would spend a lifetime making it up to her.

He awoke early in the morning, full of self-loathing, and it took him a moment or two to work out what had disturbed him at such an hour. He realised he had heard the front door close. He got out of bed and went to the window, which overlooked the square, and saw Catherine at the end of the road, dressed in her blue travelling coat, and carrying a small bag.

'No!' he exclaimed, guessing at once that she was running away. He called to his valet, barking orders for a horse to be ready on the double, and quickly dressed in his jodhpurs and riding jacket. 'Let me know the moment the horse is ready,' he said. 'Do not waste a moment!' He also guessed Catherine would not go without leaving a note for Alyssa, and that it would give him some indication of where she was going.

In his desperate state, he burst into

Catherine's bedroom, and, as he had anticipated, found the note on the dressing table. He had no compunction about reading it and hoped that Miss Alyssa would understand his urgency.

'*My dearest Alyssa,*' he read. '*For reasons I cannot say, I have to go away. I am going to remind Cousin George of his responsibilities, and hope that he will allow me to return to Willoughby Manor. I know that you and Mr Harrington will be very happy, and I wish you both all the love in the world. Please help Kitty to find another position as I am unable to take her with me. I am sorry to leave in such a way, darling, and I hope you can find it in your heart to forgive me. Tell Mr Oakley, I am sorry. He will know why. Your devoted sister, Catherine.*'

'Sorry?' he whispered. 'Catherine . . . darling . . . ' She had nothing to be sorry for. He was the fool who had frightened her away!

Even though he knew where she was going, he still found himself searching her room for more clues, whilst he waited for his horse to be ready. Under the bed he found her sketch pad, and idly flicked through it. 'Oh, my love . . . ' he murmured, as he found page after page of depictions of his own face staring back at him.

'What is happening?' Alyssa had heard the commotion and came dashing into Catherine's room.

'Catherine has run away.'

'What?'

Xander handed her the note. 'I am sorry, I know I should not have read it. But it's essential I know where she is going.'

'But she is all alone,' said Alyssa, tears filling her pretty eyes. 'Who will take care of her? Cousin George won't. He does not care about us at all. What if he throws her out onto the street?'

'I shall bring her back, Miss Alyssa, I promise,' declared Xander. 'Then we will both take care of her.'

8

Just as Xander was mounting his horse, Andrew drew up at the house in a carriage. 'Xander!' he called out urgently.

'I cannot stop, Andrew. Miss Willoughby has run away. I am going to bring her back.'

'You need to hear this. The two names Miss Willoughby gave you from the forged army documents — '

'What about them?'

'They were sisters, both dressmakers, but were accused of being enemies of the Revolution, because they had made gowns for Marie Antoinette and other ladies at the French court. They were guillotined in the first year of The Terror, Xander.'

'But who would know that unless they had a list of all those executed?' Xander pondered.

'Exactly. It's enough to make them

seem trustworthy, if they opposed the Revolution.'

'But why are they leaving for America?' mused Xander. 'Unless . . . unless they are planning to assassinate the king, then leave the country.'

'But at least now we know who to look out for at all the ports.'

'I am not so sure,' said Xander. 'In the past few days I have felt there has been someone watching the house. It may be my imagination, but my instincts are usually correct. I think we need to talk to His Majesty about cancelling the parade. It is too dangerous. I shall see to it when I return. At the present moment I am more concerned about Miss Willoughby.'

'Try not to worry too much, Xander. Miss Willoughby has a bit more about her than most young women we know.'

It was not what Xander wanted to hear. He wanted to believe that she desperately needed his care and protection — even if it was only to prevent her having to rely on Cousin George.

He galloped off in the general direction that Catherine had taken, hoping that he would easily catch up with her before she reached the coach company, but there was no sign of her. She must have walked more quickly than he imagined. When he reached the coach company he made enquiries, but was assured by the clerk that no young lady of her description had been there that morning.

It did not make sense that she would not use the nearest coach company, unless she feared being followed. He began to wonder just how upset she was, and felt his heart grow heavy. He hated to think of her wandering the streets of London in such a state. Anyone might take advantage of her.

With no real clue to where he was going, he rode through the streets near to the coach company, hoping that perhaps she had just become lost and was approaching it by a different route. Each time he traced his path back to the coach company, but they still insisted they had not seen her. As time went on, he became more and more concerned for her welfare. He was on the approach to Blackfriars Bridge, and was about to pass a man and a street urchin involved in a loud argument, when he noticed what they were fighting over. It was a blue bonnet — the one he had seen Catherine wearing that very morning.

'You're nothing but a little thief, that's what you are,' growled the man, striking out at the child.

'No, I'm not. I've got to help the lady,' cried the boy.

Xander jumped down from his horse, and stopped the man just as he was about to clip the boy around the ear. 'If you strike the child again, I shall strike you. Be on your way, sir.' As the disgruntled man shuffled away, Xander crouched down so that he was near to the boy's height. The child was very undernourished and small, but Xander guessed him to be about ten years old. 'Now — tell me about the lady who owns this hat. And I shall know straight away if you lie.'

'I am not lying, sir, honest I'm not. They took her in a carriage, and went across the bridge with her.'

'Slow down. Where did this happen? I want to know everything.' Xander's heart pounded in his chest. His instinct was to get on his horse and chase off over the bridge in hot pursuit, but he knew he had to get as much information as possible, to know what he was dealing with. 'First of all, what is your name?'

'I'm Edward, sir, but everyone calls me Ned. She was walking, sir.' He named the street on which he had seen Catherine. 'And this black carriage stops by her and a lady — an older lady with bright red hair — sticks her head out the window. They was talking nice to begin with, though I don't think the young lady liked the other one. She was all stiff, like, and not wanting to talk. Then the two men jumped off the carriage and put a sack over the young lady's head. They knocked off her bonnet, sir, and then puts her into the coach. I followed them, Sir, as fast as I could, and they come this way, towards Blackfriars Bridge. I thought if I seen where they went, I could tell someone about the young lady being ab . . . ab . . . stolen, like, and where they took her. But this man thought I'd stolen the hat, and I didn't, sir, honestly I didn't. I was just trying to help the pretty young lady.

'You see, there's men that steal pretty ladies and make them do horrible things, sir. They took my sister, Mary, and we've never seen her since. But every night Mother says a prayer for her soul, saying that she will have been forced into wickedness, but that she hopes God will forgive her.'

Xander could have done without the last piece of information. It only increased his fear for Catherine's safety. But his instinct told him otherwise. Catherine had not been taken for that reason.

'The lady with red hair, did you happen to hear her name?'

'I think the young lady said it, sir. It was Sum . . . Sum . . . Summat . . . '

'Somerson?'

'Yes, that's it, sir. There was another lady in the carriage as well, sir. I only saw her quickly. She was dressed like a maid but she was bossing everyone about like she was in charge.'

'The French maid . . . ' Xander had heard the gossip about Phoebe's maid, but had dismissed it as xenophobia. There were many French people living in England, having escaped The Terror, and not all of them were enemies.

Now he began to wonder. It could be that Phoebe was simply paying him back for dropping her, but that did not make sense. Kidnapping Catherine was too extreme for what was merely the end of a love affair.

A different picture was beginning to form, albeit hazily. The people he believed were watching the house — the rumours that Phoebe's maid liked to listen at doors. Was it all linked? Catherine's abduction, Phoebe's French maid and the attempt on the king's life? Whatever the reason for her abduction, he had to find her — and quickly.

'You are a good, brave boy,' he said now to Ned. 'You are also clever. You remember important things, and not many people do. I happen to know the Captain, and he could use clever lads like you.' The little boy seemed to grow several inches taller at his words. 'Now, I want you to do something for me. Go to my house.' Xander gave him the address. 'Ask for Mr Harrington. Can you remember that name?'

'Yes, sir. Mr Harrington.'

'Take this bonnet with you and tell Mr Harrington that it is one that belongs to Miss Willoughby.'

'Is that the pretty lady, sir?'

'That's her. Tell Mr Harrington everything you have told me, and that he is to come to Mrs Somerson's house in Surrey and bring help. I shall be waiting there for him. Are you sure you can remember all that?'

'Yes, I can, sir. I hope the young lady will be all right, sir.'

'So do I, Ned. If you do all this, you can ask Mr Harrington to give you half a crown. Mind you don't ask for any more, or the Captain will be really angry with you when I tell him.'

'I won't ask for anything, sir. I just want to help the lady.'

'Yes, you must be paid for your services. Or *I'll* be angry with you. After you have spoken to Mr Harrington, I want you to ask for Miss Alyssa, and tell her I said she is to give you some breakfast. Then tell her where you and your mother live. She is Miss Willoughby's sister, and I know they will want to call on you when Miss Willoughby is safe. Now — tell me again everything I have asked you to do.'

Ned stumbled on a few details, but he remembered the most important points. 'Good lad. Now go,' Xander urged him. 'Hurry.'

Xander galloped across Blackfriars

Bridge, hoping that he had made the right guess about where Phoebe and her maid would take Catherine. If he was wrong, the consequences did not bear thinking about.

★ ★ ★

Even without the sack covering her, Catherine had no idea where they were going. She guessed from the position of the sun that they were going south, but as she had never travelled south of London before, she had no idea what county they were in.

They travelled for about an hour and a half, before reaching an old manor house that was practically falling apart. The carriage did not go up the approach to the manor house. Instead it stopped near to the gatehouse, which was just as dirty and run-down.

'Get out,' said Celine. 'And don't even think of running away. We are miles from the nearest town.'

Catherine got out of the carriage,

closely followed by Mrs Somerson. She had hardly spoken throughout the trip. Celine was most definitely in charge of events. She led Catherine into the gatehouse and up a rickety staircase. There were two doors at the top. The maid opened one and pushed Catherine through it.

'Everything you need is in there. You have got until midnight tonight to give us the documents we require.'

'That is impossible,' said Catherine, even though she knew it would not be so difficult. 'I have no idea what to do.'

'If you are trying to stall for time, forget it. My sister may have the brains of a sparrow, but I don't.'

'Mrs Somerson is your sister?'

'Yes. She has her uses, being the one born with looks.'

Catherine felt the anger rising in her as she thought how Phoebe had misled Xander. Did they suspect even for a moment he was the Captain?

'Why are you doing this?'

The woman sneered again. 'If you

think you can stall by asking me too many questions, you're wrong.'

'No, truly, I am interested. My brother Jimmy said you had a noble cause, and I wondered if that was true.'

'As far as we are concerned, it is. Not that we gave Mr Willoughby the details. Phoebe told him we were helping some friends in France. He'd never have agreed if he'd known the truth. You have never seen the real London. The people who starve on the street whilst that coxcomb of a Prince spends fortunes on parties and women — and the king is mad, everyone knows that. It is time this government was shaken up.'

'You are going to kill the king! That's what this is about . . .'

'It will strike a blow at the heart of your government and let the paupers know that others care about them.'

'I would agree with you,' said Catherine, 'about the inequality. I am not as blind to others' suffering as you think. But I believe you are lying. I do not think you care what happens to the poor. Not after the way I saw your sister treat Kitty. Your sister has no regard for the lower classes at all.

'No, I think you are doing this purely for money, because your sister's house is falling apart to such an extent she dare not live in it, and because she wants to be part of the society you say she despises. That is her reason, anyway. I am not entirely sure about yours — though I do wonder whether you really are half-French.'

Celine smiled and bowed slightly. 'I am indeed. Phoebe is my half-sister. We have the same father, but my mother was French. He dropped her the moment he found himself a rich English wife.'

'And so you hate the English?' Catherine regarded her with contempt. 'The English as a whole are not responsible for what your father did. But I fear you enjoy the bitterness too much. Or maybe it is just the money your French masters pay you.'

Even as she spoke, Catherine wondered whether she was being entirely fair. Society did set certain expectations on people in regard to whom they married. But was French society any different? She doubted it. Those fortunate enough to be in power, as far as she knew, behaved in the same way the world over.

'That is easy for you to say, the daughter of a gentleman farmer, with a foot in society no matter how poor you are, as long as you have a rich benefactor like Mr Oakley. It's a pity, Miss Willoughby,' Celine said, changing tack slightly. 'I could quite like you in different circumstances. You are a very astute young lady. I also know you have no money either, which is why you forged that note about Mr Oakley's guardianship. Yes, I was listening at the door. Join us, and you can have all the money you could wish for. We may have different reasons for disliking this society, but there is no reason why we cannot work together to bring it to its knees.'

'Whatever my personal feelings about

excesses of the rich, I would never become involved in a plot to kill the King. Particularly as it means working for our enemies. Do you really believe your revolutionary council cares any more about the poor in France than our royalty do about the poor in Britain? The French working people are just as hungry now as they were before the Revolution began. Only the names of those in charge have changed. Their excesses still go on. And if you think you could destabilise the British monarchy by killing the king, you are very much mistaken. You forget that we have already lost one monarch to revolution, and England survived it, and brought the monarchy back.'

'Not quite as clever as I thought, then. Otherwise you would have at least pretended in order to save your life. If you are good, we will bring you food and drink later. Now get to work.' Celine left the room, slamming the door shut. Catherine heard the key turning in the lock.

Looking around properly for the first time, Catherine found herself in a tiny room with a grimy-looking truckle bed, and a chair and table. On the table lay a pile of paper, the same letter from the nobleman with an example of his handwriting, a sheet of paper bearing two more women's names, writing implements and a candle. They had thought of everything.

Despite that, Catherine found it impossible to begin work. It was not only to keep up the pretence of being unable to forge the documents. The thought that she might be contributing to the death of the king was horrifying. The idea that she had already done it unwittingly when Jimmy first brought her the work, and that it was the reason he had been silenced, was overwhelming. How naïve they had both been, to think that the only people asking for the service would be those with a noble cause. They had been stupid not to ask further questions.

Jimmy had clearly been seduced by

Mrs Somerson's charms, and probably would never have believed she could be involved in such a heinous plot. But Catherine knew that she should have pressed for more information. She had simply trusted her brother to do the decent thing.

Xander was right. What Catherine had done, not just to him with the guardianship letter, but in putting the king's life at risk, was reprehensible. If he found out that she had assisted in the assassination, he would despise her even more.

She imagined that the sisters planned to assassinate the king, then use the letters from the French nobleman to escape detection. The authorities, even if they suspected Mrs Somerson and Celine, would be looking for an Englishwoman and her maid, not two French women escaping the guillotine. Catherine had to make things right, no matter what the outcome.

She sat on the bed, despondent, and was still sitting there an hour later, when Celine returned.

'I have brought you a drink.' She handed Catherine a pewter tankard filled with water. 'Do not worry, it is not drugged. We need you awake.'

As Catherine was thirsty, she took a sip, and then grimaced at the brackish taste.

'Why have you not started on the letters?'

'I am not going to do it,' answered Catherine calmly.

'Now listen to me, you stupid girl.' Celine grabbed Catherine by the hair and dragged her to the table, knocking the tankard to the floor, and forcing her to sit on the chair. 'I can send one of the men back to London at any moment, and when he gets there, he will kill your sister.'

'He will not, because Alyssa is too well cared for.' It was something Catherine had spent the last hour considering. The rough-looking men would never be allowed anywhere near Alyssa. Harrington and Xander would see to that. She had to place her trust in them, and hope that if her sister was in danger, they would act quickly enough to prevent her being harmed. 'And even if he succeeds, at least I shall have done the right thing.'

Catherine thought of Jimmy, and how he had lost his life, and all the times that Xander, as the Captain, had risked his life to save others — including the time he refused an order from his Commanding Officer that would have led to unjustified carnage. She tried to be inspired by their courage, despite the terror in her heart. 'I am not going to help you commit regicide.'

Celine pulled a pistol from the pocket in her dress. 'I was afraid you'd say that. But I think your own instinct to live will overcome any objections you have. You have until the count of ten to start work.' She pressed the pistol against Catherine's temple.

'One . . . two . . . three . . . '

9

As Xander was able to travel across country on his horse, he reached Phoebe Somerson's house only a short time after the sisters and their prisoner did. Under the cover of a copse several hundred yards away, he could see the carriage parked outside the gatehouse, and the two men standing guard at the door. Occasionally either Phoebe or the other woman — the maid — came out to them, and they talked for a while, looking to an upper window, which had been boarded up. It gave him a good indication of where Catherine was.

He had never been to Phoebe's country house, and was surprised by how derelict the larger building was. He wondered if she and her gang had abducted Catherine in order to demand a ransom. He was tempted to approach the men and offer any terms they wanted, in order to get her back. But he had no weapon on him, and for all he knew, they might well be armed and simply open fire.

Waiting for Harrington to arrive with help was frustrating, but he knew he had no choice. It would be foolish to approach the gatehouse unprepared.

He had been waiting an agonising three-quarters of an hour when he heard the approach of hooves on the London road. He pursed his lips and let out a shrill whistle when he recognised Harrington at the head of a group of men. They had brought a carriage with them, for which he was grateful. Catherine might not be in any fit state to ride back to London.

'Xander . . . ' Harrington rode across to the copse and dismounted, making sure he kept out of sight of the gate-house. 'I've brought help, as you see. What is going on?'

'I think they want her to forge new letters.' He briefly told Harrington about the links he had made. 'Either that, or they intend to hold her to ransom. But no one has left since I arrived, and I feel sure they would send someone with a note if they wanted money. Did you bring me a weapon?'

Harrington handed over a pistol, and a sword in a scabbard, which Xander secured around his waist. 'We'll take the two men out first.'

As he spoke, a shot rang out from the direction of the gatehouse. Fearing the worst, and with no thought for his own safety, he jumped on his horse, commanding Harrington and the others to follow him. The two ruffians had no time to react to the sudden onslaught, as they also seemed shocked by the gunshot. Xander and Harrington were able to knock them out quickly, leaving the others to tie them up, whilst Xander kicked open the gatehouse door and ran inside.

Phoebe was crouching in a corner, whimpering. 'Xander . . . darling . . . ' she cried, reaching out to him. 'I had nothing to do with it. Celine made me do it. I'd never hurt dear Miss

Willoughby. I . . . '

'Phoebe, out of my way! Andrew, deal with this . . . woman.' He dashed past her and up the stairs.

Just off the landing was an open door, and he could smell the gunpowder emanating from the room. 'Catherine!' He went in, terrified of what he might find, and cursing himself for waiting for help. He should have come for her sooner. If he was too late . . .

He found her standing at the edge of the room, the pistol in her hand. She trembled from head to toe and there was a faint sheen of sweat on her forehead. 'I killed her,' she said quietly. 'I didn't mean to. I just tried to get the pistol from her because I didn't really want to die and . . . '

Celine lay in a pool of blood on the floor. Xander took a blanket from the truckle bed and threw it over her. Catherine, who had not moved in all the time he had been in the room, looked at him with wide, terrified eyes.

'I am so sorry. I did not mean to help

them in the plot against the king. I honestly did not know . . . '

'Catherine . . . ' He moved towards her, just in time to catch her as she fell into a dead faint.

Harrington came bursting into the room. 'Oh Lord, Xander, is she . . . ' He tailed off, staring at Catherine lying in Xander's arms.

'No, she is alive. She just fainted. It is not surprising, with everything she has been through.'

'Thank God she was not hurt. But then what happened? Who fired the pistol we heard?'

'The French maid is dead,' said Xander in slow and deliberate tones. 'I shot her as she was about to shoot Miss Willoughby.'

'But . . . ' Harrington paused, and then nodded. 'Yes — in fact I saw you do it with my own eyes.'

'Miss Willoughby saw nothing, because she fainted. So there is no need for the authorities to ask her questions about the shooting.'

'Yes, I agree.'

'Good man.'

'Phoebe and the two men are under arrest, and we're going to hand them over to the nearest gaol.'

'Will you take care of that, Andrew? I want to take her home.'

'To London?'

'No, I shall take her to Oakley Castle. It is more private, and I shall need to talk to her before she sees anyone from the authorities.'

* * *

Catherine felt so ashamed. She was not the fainting kind. Had she not said that to Xander? And what had she done, the moment he entered the room at the gatehouse? She'd fainted away.

She opened her eyes to find she was sitting next to him in a carriage. He had one hand on the reins and the other around her waist, holding her close to him. She was in the most wonderful place on earth, despite the fact that the movement of the carriage was making her nauseous.

She wanted to talk to him. To explain everything, and let him know that she had not given into Celine's demands, whatever he might think of her, but her mouth felt dry and her head hurt.

Her recollection of events seemed hazy. She remembered Celine starting to count to ten, and she had reached five when it suddenly struck Catherine that it was a ludicrous thing to do as it gave her time to think. Before the woman had reached ten, Catherine had gripped her hand and pushed her away. There was a struggle, as they fought for the pistol, and then, as they both fell to the floor, a loud retort.

Catherine could see herself, almost as if watching an actress on stage, getting up with the pistol in her hand and looking down at the dead woman. Then Xander arrived, and she had wanted to tell him how brave she had been. To tell him how she had stood firm, defied their demands. Only she had started to feel ill. Not least because she knew she had killed someone. Then she had disgraced herself by fainting in front of him. He was so brave; he would despise her for that, surely. But she had killed someone, and she could not rid herself of the nasty taste in her mouth.

'Xander . . . ' she whispered, as the carriage rolled through the countryside.

'Do not try to speak,' he murmured. She was not sure, but she thought he leaned over and kissed her hair. She must have imagined it, because he would never do such a thing. Not when she had been an unwitting accomplice in a plot against King George's life.

She did not know how long they had been travelling when Oakley Castle came into view. She had dozed for part of the journey, fighting the fever that had gripped her. She supposed, as they approached the house, that he had brought her here because he was too ashamed to take her to London again. With that came the dreadful realisation that everyone knew what she had done.

Certainly it would not matter to her if no one wanted her in society — but it might harm Alyssa.

'We're home, darling,' said Xander, as the carriage halted outside the house. 'You are safe. No one can hurt you again.'

Catherine wondered who 'darling' was. She was sure no one else had travelled with them. Had he brought Mrs Somerson back, too? What if he did not know about her? There was so much she had to tell him, if only she had the energy to speak. Catherine glanced around and could see no one else, so the mystery remained.

Xander went around to her side of the carriage, to help her down.

'No,' she croaked. 'I can manage on my own. I am able to walk.'

He ignored her and helped her down anyway. She pulled away from him, determined to show that she was not some weak, insipid woman. She could stand on her own two feet. Except that her feet seemed to be made of jelly. She was going to faint, and she could not do that in front of him. Not again. He despised her enough already.

'I am quite capable of . . . ' she tried to say, but the world started to spin.

His arms went around her and she heard him shouting. Was he angry with her? She could not blame him, even if it was rather unkind of him to shout when her head hurt so much. But he also seemed to be shouting at Griffiths and a physician.

She decided to have one last try at showing him she could walk, and of proving it to him, but then blackness descended and she could not say anything at all.

What followed were nightmares, as she relived over and over the dreadful scene with Celine. She had killed someone, and even if that person had been evil, she did not deserve to die. Then firm but gentle hands lifted her and offered her a drink, but she pushed it away, because she knew that the water was dirty, and it would make her even more unwell. A deep voice entreated her to trust him, and instinctively she did, taking the water offered. It tasted wonderful, clean and fresh. But still her illness persisted.

Then the vision changed and she was floating upwards, and looked down to see her sister crying at the side of a bed. There was someone lying in the bed, but Catherine couldn't make out who it was. Was it Celine? Perhaps she had not died after all. But Catherine was sure she had, and that even if she was alive, Alyssa would not be crying over her.

'No, Alyssa, don't cry,' she whispered. 'Harrington will take care of you.' And she was glad to see that Harrington was there, holding Alyssa in his arms. She had done everything she could for her sister, and it was time to let go. Only something . . . someone . . . kept pulling her back. The same, safe, strong arms that brought her the fresh water. She wanted to go to sleep and find peace, but they kept insisting she drink water and eat broth.

'Please don't leave me,' she heard the deep voice murmur. 'Not when I have so much to say to you.'

'I am so tired,' she breathed.

'I know, darling. But you have to fight for a little while longer.'

So she fought, because he had asked her to and she wanted to please him. And then finally, the peace she sought came, and she rested on his shoulder and fell asleep, exhausted from the fight.

She opened her eyes to see sunlight streaming into the bedroom, and Kitty bustling around her. 'Oh, Miss Willoughby!' Kitty approached the bed. 'You're awake.' Her maid gave her a broad smile. 'We've all been so worried about you. I'm ever so glad you're well again. Mr Oakley said it was that horrible dirty place they took you to that did it. It gave you a fever.'

'It was the water,' said Catherine. 'I should not have drunk it. Where am I, Kitty?' Catherine looked around the bedroom, but failed to recognise it.

'You are at Oakley Castle, Miss Willoughby. We all are. Mr Oakley said we all had to come back from London because . . . well, it is not important now. You are well again, and that is all that matters. Mr Oakley said I am not to upset you with talking about things what might have happened. Mr Oakley and Miss Alyssa, they haven't wanted to leave your side for a minute. But last night the physician said your fever had broken, and Mr Harrington ordered them both to get some rest. Otherwise they would have been here when you woke up, I'm sure.

'Then Mr Oakley and Mr Harrington had to go off to London early to talk about those villains. Fancy someone wanting to kill the king. It's horrible. Oh! I hope they hang them, Miss Willoughby.'

'This is not my room,' observed Catherine, wanting to think about anything but hanging. The walls were a cheerful primrose pattern, with silk covers on the four-poster bed to match.

'No, Mr Oakley put you in the room right next to his, so he could watch over you, he says. It was his mother's room when she was alive.'

Before Catherine could find time to digest that information, the bedroom door opened, and Alyssa burst in. 'Oh, darling!' she cried, running to the bed and throwing her arms around Catherine. 'We thought we had lost you.'

'Now, Miss Alyssa,' admonished Kitty, 'you know Mr Oakley says we are not to upset Miss Willoughby with all the details.'

'I am fine, Kitty, don't worry,' said Catherine. 'I can guess for myself that I have been very ill.' Kitty curtseyed and left the room.

'How long have I been ill, Alyssa?' asked Catherine.

'Over a week, dearest.'

'And the king? Is he safe?'

'Oh yes, do not worry. They cancelled the parade.'

Catherine wondered just how much trouble she was in. She felt sure that

Mrs Somerson would have told the authorities that she, Catherine, was the one who had forged the first false letters, not Jimmy. Added to the fact that she had killed a woman. Was it possible she had survived the fever only to have to face the gallows for treason and murder?

10

You are still unwell, dearest,' remarked Alyssa, when Catherine shivered involuntarily. 'Try to get some rest, and I shall come back to see you after breakfast.' Alyssa pulled the coverlet around her sister's shoulders and walked to the door, looking back to blow her a kiss.

'Alyssa . . . did Mr Oakley say anything about the authorities wishing to speak to me?'

'No, darling. Why would they want to do that?'

'I killed someone, Alyssa. Mrs Somerson's sister, Celine.'

'No, you did not, dearest. Mr Oakley said he heard you talking in your sleep, and from what you said, he thought you might have had a dream that you had killed someone. He warned us that you might think some of the dreams really happened, because a fever can make imaginary things seem very vivid, but you have not killed anyone, dearest. The very thought of you doing such a thing! Now get some rest.'

Catherine could not rest. After Alyssa had gone, she got out of bed, feeling a little shaky, but stronger than she had been when Xander brought her back to Oakley Castle. She called for Kitty to draw a bath, and lay soaking in it, revelling in the clean, warm water, even though her mind was still troubled.

If she had dreamed about killing Celine, whilst in the fever, what else had she imagined? Had it been her mind that conjured up Xander holding her in his arms and talking to her so tenderly, begging her to live because he had so much to say to her? Had she merely imagined the things she wished he would say to her, if he loved her as she loved him?

Kitty said that he had put her in the primrose room to watch over her, but that might have been so that she did not run away before the authorities could speak to her. She would not flee again. She would face up to whatever happened, even if the idea made her feel weak at the knees.

After she had eaten breakfast in her room, she found she could not bear the thought of getting back into bed. She dressed and went downstairs. Griffiths was in the hallway.

'Miss Willoughby, it is good to see you up and about again,' he said. 'Miss Alyssa is in the morning room with Mr Oakley's aunt.'

'I think I should like to go out for a walk,' said Catherine, half-expecting him to block her exit. Instead, he opened the front door.

'Are you sure you are well enough, Miss Willoughby? I could ask one of the maids to walk behind you, in case you feel poorly again.'

Griffith's kindness made Catherine want to cry. She sensed the offer was genuinely made, and not an excuse to keep an eye on her movements.

'Mr Oakley will not be very pleased if

he returns and finds we have not looked after you properly,' the butler added.

'I shall be fine, thank you, Griffiths. I won't go very far. I just need some fresh air after being in the sick room for so long.'

'Very well, Miss Willoughby. But do take care. We have all been very worried about you, if you don't mind me saying.'

'Not at all. You are kind.'

Catherine walked to the oak tree under which she had sat to complete her painting of Oakley Castle. The weather had changed for the better, and it was a bright, mild spring day. She breathed in the fresh air, wishing she had brought her sketch pad with her, and then remembered that she had left it behind in London.

Even though she had not walked far, she felt suddenly tired, so she sat down in the grass and leaned her back against the tree. She closed her eyes, and thought back over everything that had happened. She *did* shoot Celine, she was sure of it. Or perhaps she wanted to believe it — because if she had not imagined that, then she could not have imagined Xander caring for her in the way he had whilst she was ill.

'Catherine!'

She opened her eyes to see Xander crouched down beside her. His hand felt heavy, but comforting, on her shoulder.

'Thank God,' he said. 'I was afraid you had fainted. Why on earth have they let you come out here alone? I told them to take care of you.'

'I was not going to run away,' she said, sitting up.

'I should hope not.' He smiled tenderly, and it seemed to Catherine that the sun shone a little brighter. 'And if you had done, I would have found you and brought you back.'

'I am willing to face up to what I have done,' she said in a sombre voice. 'I suppose the authorities wish to speak to me.'

'What about?'

'Killing Celine, for a start. But they are probably more interested in me taking part in a plot to kill the king.'

'And when exactly did you do all this?'

'You know when. Even if you have managed to convince Alyssa I did not kill Celine, I know what happened. And you cannot possibly put the first lot of forged letters down to my fevered imagination.'

'No, probably not.'

'And I am sure Mrs Somerson will tell them about it.'

'Mrs Somerson told the authorities that she'd approached your brother, and then she had some ridiculous notion that you were a master forger and not Jimmy. She said her sister told her she had overheard you admitting to it. But I pointed out, quite reasonably I think, that not only was that hearsay, so inadmissible in court, the very idea of a nineteen-year-old girl of impeccable character, who had been brought up quietly in the country, having the talent and the criminal inclination to do such a thing was ridiculous. And they agree with me. The King himself says it is ludicrous, and he has the final word on it. In fact, having known of Mr Willoughby's valiant work with the Captain, His Majesty even refuses to believe he was involved. He is somehow convinced that Jimmy suspected the plot and was investigating it.'

Catherine did not have to wonder who put that idea into the king's head. 'Did they not wonder why I was abducted? And please do not try to convince me I imagined *that* because of my fever. I am growing bored with that excuse already. Mrs Somerson will have told them.'

'As I said, Mrs Somerson and her sister had this notion you were a forger, hence the abduction.'

'They might think that is evidence.'

'Catherine, Phoebe Somerson is a woman who will say anything to talk herself out of trouble. She has said it is all her sister's fault, which is convenient because her sister is dead and cannot speak for herself.'

'Actually I think that part might be true. The sister was definitely the mastermind behind the plot.'

'Accepted. But then she said you were involved, which, as we have established, is ludicrous. Added to which, she tried to impugn the character of a brave, noble young man who not only lost his life recently but who was known to have helped hundreds of people escape from France. All whilst she was plotting to kill the King. Who on earth is going to listen to her?'

'How did you do manage to do that?' asked Catherine, as relief flooded through her, not only that she would not be charged, but that Jimmy's memory would not be tainted. 'Why would you convince them? It was for Jimmy, I suppose.'

'Of course. It does mean you will have to behave yourself in future. No more forgery. Otherwise the Captain is going to spend all his time breaking you out of jail, and I am going to spend all my time lying to the King.'

Catherine missed the significance of his words. 'I shall never undertake anything like that again. I promise. I do not think Jimmy or I ever thought of what it might lead to.' She hugged her arms around herself. 'It was fun, helping the Captain, because we knew it was for a wonderful cause. But we were stupid. We did not ask enough questions when the new work came in.'

'Jimmy did not ask enough questions. You were not wrong to trust him, as you had trusted him before. He should have made more checks.'

'Are you really angry with him? About Mrs Somerson, I mean? Because she was your . . . ' Catherine hunted around for the proper word and failed, 'lady . . . and he and she . . . '

Xander, who had been crouching for some time, turned around and sat on the grass, with his back against the tree, next to Catherine. He stretched out his long legs, and crossed them at the ankles. 'I might have been, if I had known at the time. My pride would have certainly been hurt, if not my heart. If he had come to me, and told me, man to man, that he loved her, then as I considered him to be my brother, I would have stood back. Jimmy paid for his mistake in a way I would never have wanted. She was never worth that price. Not to me.'

'I thought you loved her.'

'No. I have only ever been in love once in my life.'

'Oh.' Catherine did not even want to ask who the lucky lady was. 'I am sorry I deceived you, with the guardianship letter. I misjudged you, and I was hurt and angry about Jimmy's death. I can understand if you are still angry.'

'Did I ever tell you about the time Jimmy and I helped some nobles escape from France?'

'No.' Catherine frowned, wondering where the discussion was going.

'It was the hardest job we ever had to do. We had to travel one hundred miles on foot, and did not eat for days. A few times we thought the game was up and we'd be sure to die. One night, we were trapped in a barn, surrounded by Frenchies who were slowly moving in on us, and Jimmy said to me, 'Xander, I want you to promise me that if I die, you will take care of Catherine and Alyssa and be their guardian'. So whether he had written the note or not, it only confirmed what he had already asked me.'

'You are such a liar.' Catherine smiled, but at the same time she felt tears stinging her eyes.

'You doubt the poignant story I have just told you? You disbelieve the word of a gentleman and man of honour?' Xander affected incredulity.

'No! You are only saying it because you are a gentleman and man of honour, and for that I bless you.'

'I am not lying, and I resent the implication.' Xander paused. 'He also said, 'and make sure Catherine has some pretty dresses, because that black one with the darned sleeve looks terrible on her'.'

'And you say women chatter! It's a wonder, with a conversation lasting that long, that the French didn't find you in that barn.' Catherine hardly believed that after so much anguish and fear she would be able to laugh so easily. 'Did he read passages from the Bible too? Lead you in a rousing chorus of battle hymns?'

'Jimmy was my brother at arms, Catherine,' Xander said more seriously. 'He might not have asked me to care for you and Alyssa, but that was probably because he knew without having to ask that I would.'

'You are really not angry with me any more?'

'I never was.'

'But you said . . . '

'I know what I said. It was my clumsy way of trying to protect you. I thought that if I made you feel ashamed, you would never do anything like it again, and then you would be safe. I should never have said the things I did. Will you forgive me?'

'Forgive you? There's nothing to forgive. I was the one who . . . '

'Took care of your sister when no one else would,' Xander said emphatically. 'I cannot pretend I do not wish you would have trusted me to help you both when Jimmy died, but given the impression you had of me, from the opinion I have allowed society to hold, I can hardly blame you.'

As he spoke, Alyssa and Harrington came out of Oakley Castle and walked along the terrace, arm in arm, closely followed by Aunt Harriet, who strolled behind with a beatific smile on her face. They waved to Xander and Catherine, who waved back.

'I hope it is acceptable to you,' said Xander, 'but I have told them they need not wait out the Season to marry. Andrew has been Alyssa's rock these past few days, and I know she loves him more than ever.'

'I am very happy for them,' murmured Catherine. 'And it will be delightful to attend a wedding, after all the pain of the past months.'

'Yes — a double wedding, in fact.'

'A *double* wedding?' Catherine felt a cold hand grip her heart.

'Oh yes, I have not yet told you, have I? Of course I have had to assure His Majesty that your name will not be mentioned in any further scandals, and the best way to do that was to find you a husband. Which I have. If you think he's good enough for you.'

Catherine jumped up from the ground, feeling her head spin as she did so. But she was stronger than before, and relieved to know that she was not going to faint. 'No!' she cried, turning towards the house.

Xander leapt up and followed her, catching her arm and whirling her around. '*No?*'

'I do not wish to marry anyone, because there is no one who could be good enough for me. At least, not the one I want. I love you, and whilst I know you might never love me because of the things I have done ... even though you have been wonderfully kind and understanding about it all ... I cannot bear the thought of being another man's wife when I love you so dearly. I had rather go away, and live alone, than ... '

Before Catherine could say anything more, Xander had pulled her into his arms and was ardently kissing her lips, her cheeks, her forehead, her nose, and then her lips again.

'Do you really think I would trust anyone but the Captain to keep you out of trouble?' he demanded, when he had reluctantly stopped kissing her. She clung to him, afraid that she really might faint then, even though the spinning in her head was a much more pleasurable sensation than before.

'Darling Catherine, when I found out they had taken you, and then when you were ill, I thought I had lost you before I could beg for your forgiveness for how badly I treated you. I prayed to God, every night you were ill, that He would give me the chance to tell you how much I love you.'

'You do?'

'More than life itself. Why do you think I wanted you to stop doing the forgeries?'

'Because it is illegal and immoral?'

'Well, yes, there is that. Though looking at you, it's hard to believe you're capable of being either. But also because Jimmy learned the hard way that not everyone can be trusted. The thought of you being hurt . . . as you so nearly were . . . ' He held her to him more tightly still.

'But when you kissed me in the garden at Oakley Mansion, I thought you despised me because I allowed you to do so.'

'No, I was disgusted with myself for taking advantage of you. You are so young, Catherine, and Phoebe kept calling me your father, which made me worry about the age difference between us. I wanted you to have a chance to find someone of your own age.'

'I don't care about our ages. I don't want anyone else, Xander. Only you.'

'And I only want you, my love. I realised that when I saw you walking away from Oakley Mansion. I told you I'd only ever been in love once. I was talking about you, my darling.'

She gasped. 'Do you really mean that?'

'Every word. And I am not going to do anything to put you at risk again. The Captain has hung up his mask. The war will be over soon anyway, so he will not be needed for much longer.'

'I am afraid the Captain might get bored with me.' Catherine laid her head on his shoulder, feeling as if she had finally come home.

He kissed her forehead and chuckled. 'On the contrary, I have a feeling you will be one of his most challenging missions.'

'I fully intend to be.' She smiled up at him mischievously. 'To make sure you are never again tempted by the Pheobe Summersons of this world.'

'Never.' He stroked her cheek tenderly, then kissed her deeply for a long time. Finally he raised his head slightly, and murmured against her lips, 'Why would I seek an imitation of love, when I can hold the original in my arms?'

THE END

We do hope that you have enjoyed reading this large print book.

Did you know that all of our titles are available for purchase?

We publish a wide range of high quality large print books including:
Romances, Mysteries, Classics
General Fiction
Non Fiction and Westerns

Special interest titles available in large print are:
The Little Oxford Dictionary
Music Book, Song Book
Hymn Book, Service Book

Also available from us courtesy of Oxford University Press:
Young Readers' Dictionary
(large print edition)
Young Readers' Thesaurus
(large print edition)

For further information or a free brochure, please contact us at:
Ulverscroft Large Print Books Ltd.,
The Green, Bradgate Road, Anstey,
Leicester, LE7 7FU, England.
Tel: (00 44) **0116 236 4325**
Fax: (00 44) **0116 234 0205**

Other titles in the
Linford Romance Library:

BOHEMIAN RHAPSODY

Serenity Woods

Elfie Summers is an archaeologist with a pet hate of private collectors. Cue Gabriel Carter, a self-made millionaire. He invites Elfie to accompany him to Prague to verify the authenticity of an Anglo-Saxon buckle, said to grant true love to whoever touches it. And whilst Gabriel's sole motive is to settle an old score, Elfie just wants to return to her quiet, scholarly life — but the city and the buckle have other ideas . . .

LOVE AND CHANCE

Susan Sarapuk

When schoolteacher Megan bumps into a gorgeous Frenchman in the Hall of Mirrors at Versailles, she thinks she will never see him again. Until the Headteacher asks her to visit Lulu Santerre, a pupil who is threatening not to return to school. Megan discovers that Lulu's brother Raphael is the man she met at Versailles . . . When Lulu goes missing Raphael and Megan are thrown together and both of them have to make decisions about their future.